MAKE MINE A RANGER

KATE ASTER

Cover design: The Killion Group, Inc.

DEDICATION

...and one for the Airborne Ranger in the sky.

PROLOGUE

THREE YEARS AGO

The scream Tyler heard on the other side of that door could have shattered glass.

This wasn't the way he had planned on spending his Spring Break, holed up on the Labor and Delivery floor of the hospital listening to sounds no single guy like himself was ready to hear. But the girl he'd seen in the coffee shop sure didn't look any more ready to face the realities of childbirth than he was.

She was too young. Too alone.

Too much like he remembered his sister being, way back when.

Last autumn, he had been selected to be one of West Point's exchange students to the U.S. Naval Academy, spending the semester in Annapolis rather than up north. The place had grown on him, with its sail boating, pub crawls, and mild winter. When he headed back up to West Point in January, just in time for what cadets referred to as The Gloom Period—the most brutal, tedious part of winter there on the banks of the Hudson River—it seemed a pretty damn good idea to return to Annapolis for a week in the spring.

Till he had seen Bess, a friend of one of his Naval Academy instructors, sitting in the coffee shop, looking like she was just about to pop. Literally.

Before he knew it, she had gone into labor and he was driving her to the hospital.

What else could he have done? She had no husband at her side. No boyfriend within sight. It was natural he'd feel a sense of obligation to hang out with her until her friends arrived. But if he'd been smart, if he'd been like any other cadet he knew, he would have bolted the minute her friends showed up.

He could walk right now. He barely knew Bess. No one would judge him poorly for it. Bess had her two best friends in that room with her.

But for some damn reason or another, he wanted to make sure she was okay. He was never one to bail on a mission. Even in the two years he had been enlisted in the Army before getting accepted to West Point, he had gotten a reputation for tenacity in the field.

"Aaaaaaaaaaaaa-ohhh-it-hurts!"

The hairs on his arms stood on end at her cry, and his stomach roiled.

Never. Never would he put a woman through this. Didn't matter how much he liked kids, he was ready to make an appointment to get snipped first thing tomorrow.

Vasectomy, here I come.

"Push!" someone shouted on the other side of the door, followed by another blood curdling scream from Bess.

Tyler crossed his legs.

Hell with that. I think my balls just snipped themselves.

A nurse stepped out of Bess's room.

"Excuse me, Ma'am," Tyler asked. "Can't they give her something for the pain?"

The nurse shrugged. "She didn't want an epidural. And it's too late for her to change her mind now. Are you the father?"

Tyler eyed her, dumbfounded. If he were the father, wouldn't he be in there holding her hand right now as she tried to squeeze a watermelon through a keyhole? "No, Ma'am. I'm just a friend."

"Oh. Well, it shouldn't be much longer now." She gave a curt nod and stalked down the hall.

Another order to push followed by a splintering scream poured out of the room and down the hallway. And another. And another. Tyler's insides were screwing up like he had just eaten an MRE for breakfast. Normally, he had been trained to charge in when someone was suffering. Not cower in the hall helpless. This was totally out of his comfort zone.

Then he heard it—a baby's cry. Not nearly as loud as Bess's, but still, definitely a healthy set of lungs on the kid.

Heaving a sigh of relief, Tyler leaned back on his hard chair, letting his shoulders sag. It was over. Thank God. He hadn't felt this stressed jumping from a C130 in Airborne School.

Only a few minutes passed before Maeve, one of Bess's friends, stepped out of the room. Her cheeks were streaked with tears. The happy kind, Tyler guessed.

"Do you want to see the baby, Tyler?"

He hesitated. "I'm good out here."

"Come on," she urged. "She's beautiful. Bess wants to show her off."

Curiosity overtook him and he rose from his chair. Why

not? He had come this far. He should at least take a peek at the little kid.

Stepping into the room, his eyes fell immediately to the tiny baby, almost looking surreal to him. She was so small. Too small. "Is she all right?" Tyler asked, even knowing it was a stupid question as it passed from his lips. But she looked so fragile, swaddled in a yellow blanket, eyes pressed shut and skin moist and ruddy.

He couldn't take his eyes off her.

"She's fine. She's perfect." It wasn't even until she spoke to him that he noticed Bess, brow drenched with sweat, and arms holding her baby protectively.

Wow. Start off the day as a party of one, and end the day as a mom. Crazy world.

"Congratulations, Bess." Tyler tried to look at her directly as he spoke, but his eyes were still drawn to the vulnerable little girl she held. "She's beautiful. So tiny."

"Do you want to hold her?"

Hell, no.

Hell, yeah.

He could handle an M240 like it was an extension of his own arm. But could he dare to hold something so fragile, even for a moment?

At Bess's nod, Maeve took the baby from her and gently handed her to Tyler.

"Just be sure to support the head."

Tyler nodded. He knew that, remembering it from when his teenage sister had given birth. Tyler had only been five at the time. He could almost hear his mother's patient voice instructing him, an echo from years past. "Support the baby's head, Tyler."

Okay, Mom.

The baby's eyes were shut, and her face was puffy like a rosy, pink marshmallow. Lips forming a tiny o, garbled sounds came from her mouth. Not quite cries. Not quite coos. Just strange, unintelligible sounds that made Tyler crack a smile.

A little hand poked out from beneath the blanket and grasped Tyler's finger. His breath caught from the contact, and a lump lodged firmly in his throat.

"What's her name?" he asked, his eyes never leaving the baby.

"Abigail," Bess answered.

"Abigail," he repeated, his voice barely a whisper, and his eyes transfixed by the sight of her tiny fist coiled around his index finger. *That's right, little girl. You hold on to me. I've got your six.*

Her eyes opened slightly, like little windows to her soul, and locked on his gaze.

And he was lost to her.

CHAPTER 1

TODAY

It's not him. It's not him.

Bess glanced again into her rear view mirror at the red Lotus Elise sports car they had passed at the intersection. In her mind, she could still see every contour of the face through the windshield as though his outline were etched into her brain. He was wearing dark sunglasses, but Bess could feel his eyes burrowing into her as her car passed.

The hair looked like Dan's—short and sandy blonde. A little spiky on the top. The lips were a straight, thin line, hinting of displeasure.

She had seen that look on his face often enough in the months they had been together during college, the same expression that was often followed by a strike to her face.

But the car behind her was a Lotus. It had been nearly four years since she had seen Dan, and it was possible he replaced the Ford pickup he had gotten from his dad. But a flashy sports car just wasn't his style.

Of course, styles can change over four years.

No, she thought, giving her head a slight shake. It had to be her imagination again. That was it. Her lack of sleep was causing her mind to play tricks on her.

In her rear-view mirror, she saw the car turn and head in the opposite direction. "Good," she said under her breath. It was much more palatable to think she was just losing her mind than to think that Dan had found her here in Annapolis.

"What's good, Mama?" Abigail asked from the back seat.

Bess bit her lip, unaware that she had spoken so loudly. She'd have to watch that. "It's good we missed that red light. We're going to be late enough as it is."

She glanced at the clock on her dashboard. Just once, she'd love to arrive somewhere with Abigail on time. But there was always some kind of drama attached to loading her three-year-old into the car.

Picturing poor Tyler, she laughed a little, imagining the tough Army Ranger waiting for them alone, surrounded by screaming children and a throng of drooling moms wondering why a guy so hot was sitting by himself at Pirate Pop's Pizza Palace.

Tyler, she reminded herself. *Think about Tyler.* If he wasn't enough to get her mind off the imaginary image of her abusive ex-boyfriend following her around, then there was something seriously wrong with her.

The last time she had seen Tyler was a little over a year ago, when he stopped by for a quick visit on his way driving from Fort Drum to his next Army post, a coveted assignment to the 1st Ranger Battalion in Savannah. They traded a couple emails since then, and he had called on Abby's third birthday, stunned to discover that Bess's little girl was talking so much now.

Gazing in the rear view mirror, Bess smiled at the reflection of her daughter, watching the trees as they zipped along Route 2 heading north of Annapolis. Pirate Pop's was just outside of town, where the historic structures of Maryland's state capital gave way to more industrial buildings and strip malls. This was where moms like Bess spent their time—frequenting the bounce houses, little kid gyms with foam pits, and restaurants that boasted talking mechanical animals.

There was no plausible reason for a guy like Tyler to be spending a nice summer day in this part of town with her and her daughter. He should be downtown, hanging out in one of Annapolis's pubs or watching a boat race off Horn Point. Bess imagined Tyler kept in touch all these years because two of her best friends, Mick Riley and Jack Falcone, outranked him.

But whatever the reason, she was grateful that Abby had another man to add to her roster of honorary uncles.

Bess reached for the soda that was in her cup holder, desperately needing the caffeine. She hadn't yet gotten used to sleeping in the house with only the company of her little girl. Every innocuous sound—the creak of Abby's bed as she rolled over, the scratch of a bush against the siding, the clunk of the refrigerator icemaker as it kicked on—sent her heart into palpitations.

She had been spoiled all these years, living in a little Cape Cod style house with a view of the Chesapeake Bay that was owned by her friend, Maeve. When Maeve moved out to live with her new husband Jack down in Little Creek, Virginia, Bess's friend Lacey had moved in so that she could be close to her husband, Mick, who had been going through treatment for Traumatic Brain Injury at Walter Reed in Bethesda.

Now that Mick had recovered enough to go back to active duty, he and Lacey had bought a condo in DC, leaving Bess and Abby in the house alone.

Even with the security system turned on, Bess still felt like she was a target, so alone in that house with her daughter. Alone and vulnerable.

Paranoid. That's what she was. But with her history, how could she not be?

"Can I play skeeball?" Abby called out from the back seat.

"Of course. And you can ride the horse, too."

"That's for babies. It's not a real horse."

Bess laughed, remembering how much the mechanical horse had amused her daughter last time. "You used to like it."

"I'm grown up now."

"You're three, honey. Don't grow up on me too fast, okay?"

"Okay, Mama."

The conversation bolstered Bess. Until just recently, Abby barely had spoken a word, causing Bess to worry endlessly. Now, it was hard to get her daughter to keep quiet.

She glanced in her rear view mirror again, half expecting the red car to reappear with Dan's face staring at her from behind the wheel. But it was a Jeep. A Jeep never looked so good to her.

Twice now, she had seen someone who could pass as Dan's twin. The first time, she spotted him jogging down her street. He even slowed to glance at her house—she'd swear on her life that he did—then disappeared around the corner.

It was absurd, of course. In the months they had been together, Dan hadn't once gone jogging. It had to be someone who just looked like him.

But now... she thought she'd seen him again.

Shaking her head, she slowed to a stop as the light in front of her turned red. She just needed some sleep.

And a housemate. What she wouldn't give to have another responsible adult in that house, preferably one with a black belt in karate.

She flicked on her turn signal and pulled into the parking lot.

"Is Tyler giving me presents?"

Bess sighed. It was a natural question, she imagined, since most of the times Tyler's name came up it usually had a gift or two attached to it.

"Honey, it's not your birthday," Bess answered.

"I know. But he always gets me presents."

"Well, he sends those on holidays and birthdays, honey. Today is just an ordinary day." Bess half smiled. Ordinary? Not by a long shot. There was nothing ordinary about a day when she got to have lunch with a deliciously hot Army Ranger. Actually, going out with *any* man would be classified as something of a miracle. Being a single mom, it was a little hard to date a man, especially when her last relationship had caused her so much pain.

Her phone buzzed in her purse just as she was pulling into a parking space. A message from Tyler popped up on the screen. "Where are you?" he wrote. "Everything okay?"

"Just pulled into the lot. Sorry," she quickly wrote back, adding a frowning emoticon.

As she undid Abby's car seat buckle, a man emerged through the door of Pirate Pop's, his shoulders filling up the doorframe and his smile making the high noon sun seem dull in comparison.

Tyler.

Her heart did a backflip, and she reminded herself for the twentieth time today that he was really here to see Abby, not her. Not her, in her stretchy tank dress that hid the twenty

11

extra pounds of pregnancy weight that had never disappeared. Or her cheap drug store makeup that was always put on in a rush, or her sensible flip-flops that she actually considered a step up from the grubby sneakers she usually wore. Even if Bess owned a pair of sexy stilettos, she would have left them at home. Who can chase after a three-year-old in stilettos?

Abby broke into a full gallop toward Tyler as he approached. To her, Tyler was a gift-bearing superman.

Setting down a shopping bag on the pavement, he lifted Abby and swung her around.

"You're getting big, Abby," he said, the mere sound of his voice making Bess's backbone tingle, like it always did. She loved his voice.

"I'm free now," Abby responded, her "th" still sounding like "f."

"I know. Don't grow up on me too fast, okay?" he replied.

Abby laughed gleefully. "That's what Mama said in the car."

His eyes were drawn to Bess now, and his gaze on her made her blood sizzle like frying bacon on Sunday morning.

"Hey, Bess," he said, putting Abby down. "You look great."

Bess suppressed a snort of disbelief as he stole her into a hug. She nearly passed out from the sensation. The body behind his innocuous polo shirt and cargo shorts was rock hard. "You do, too."

He took Abby's hand. "Glad you got here. All the moms in there are giving me some strange looks. I think half of them think I'm some kind of freak sitting by myself. It's not exactly a place for a lone guy to hang, you know?"

"Oh, I don't think that's why they're staring," Bess enlightened him. "They may all be haggard moms like me, but they're not too tired to check out a guy with biceps like yours, Tyler."

He laughed. "Is that it?"

"I guarantee it." She smiled. "Being in the Rangers has certainly agreed with you."

"Well, glad to hear it. I was afraid it just made me a bitter, scarred up Soldier from it."

Concern creased Bess's brow. "Scars? Did something happen on one of your missions?"

Tyler shrugged. "Nothing I can't handle," he said carelessly as he herded Abby through the door. "Come on in, sweetness," he said... to Abby, Bess reminded herself. Not to her. "I got a present for you."

The air conditioning in Pirate Pop's slapped Bess as Tyler opened the door for her. The chill would help her stay awake, and maybe suppress the rising temperature underneath her skin that always seemed to accompany being near Tyler, her unattainable crush for nearly four years now.

They ordered a pizza at the counter and Tyler pulled a new stuffed toy from a shopping bag for Abby. "It's a bulldog, Abby. They're really into bulldogs down in Savannah."

Holding the dog in her grasp, Abby wrapped her arms around Tyler's leg. "Thank you," she said.

Bess's heart cracked a little at the sight of her little girl, so enraptured by the burly, adorable saint she hugged ferociously. What Bess wouldn't give for her little girl to have a father like Tyler.

"Here." Tyler handed Abby a fist full of tokens. "Go try some skeeball while your mom and I wait for the pizza." He patted her on the head before she darted away.

"So how long are you in town for?" Bess asked as she planted herself in a booth near the skeeball.

"A year, actually."

Bess's eyes opened wide. "What?"

"I'm up as an augmentee to Fort Meade."

Bess gave her head a quick shake. "But I thought you said you were going to stay in the Rangers for a while."

"I'm still part of the Battalion. They need a Ranger in a Military Intelligence position for a year. Then I'm headed back to Savannah."

"That's great." She was just happy to have another friend in Annapolis, she tried to convince herself. It had nothing to do with the way his smile made her melt like a snow cone in August heat. It might be nice to see him more than once a year just to remind herself that she still had some estrogen pumping in her blood.

"Yeah. But I've got just two days to find an apartment or I'll be stuck living on base."

Bess bit her lip, her mind wandering to the two empty rooms in her house. No way he'd want to live with a single mom and a three-year-old. But it was nice to imagine. She might actually get over the fear of Dan showing up at her door with a guy like Tyler sleeping in the same house.

With those pecs, he'd be better protection than a set of Dobermans, and a lot less risky to Abby than a couple of angry dogs.

The thud of a skeeball smacking against Plexiglas drew her eyes to Abigail. "Roll the ball, honey. Don't throw it."

Shoulders slumped, Abby frowned as she came back to the table. "I never get better," she moped.

"You just need some practice. Let me help," he offered. Without another word he got up from his seat and took Abby back to the skeeball. He bent over to slide a token into the machine, showing off the remarkable ass showcased in his cargo shorts. Good Lord. Bess swallowed a sigh. Yeah, definitely wouldn't be a good idea to be living with *that*. She'd die from unrequited lust within six weeks, tops.

She watched him take the skeeball and lift it backwards very slowly so that Abby could see the arching line of his arm as he rolled the ball onto the machine. What he didn't realize was that the slow motion movement accentuated the rigid lines of his triceps, drawing the attention of at least three nearby moms.

Bess cracked a smile. Yep, ladies, he's with me, she wanted to boast. Even though he wasn't really "with her," she could at least enjoy the moment.

Seemed his time with the Rangers had definitely added more bulk to his frame. The muscular bulk, not the soft and squishy kind that Bess had reluctantly gained since becoming a mom, putting guys like Tyler even further out of her reach.

As the server brought out the pizza, Bess frowned at the fat calories staring at her.

"Pizza's here," she called out just as Abby rolled the ball smack into a 5000 point hole.

Jumping, the little girl's ponytails bounced as she let out a squeal. "I did it! Mama, did you see?"

"Awesome, honey!"

Grabbing Tyler's hand, Abby dragged him back to the hard seats of the booth, and curled up her lip at the sight of pepperoni and sausage on one side of the pizza. "This side is mine," she said possessively, pointing to the cheese-only side. Abby had recently declared she was a vegetarian when Bess had offered her sausage one morning and she responded, "I like pigs, Mama. I don't eat them."

Bess reached into her purse. "Hands," she ordered, as Abby automatically extended her hands so that she could squirt some hand sanitizer on them. "Want some?" she asked Tyler.

"I embrace germs," he said playfully.

Bess narrowed her eyes. "Not around my kid, you won't. Hands," she repeated firmly.

"Yes, Ma'am," he said with a dramatic sigh and turned to Abby. "You've got a good mama, Abby."

That was probably the best compliment a man could have possibly given Bess. "I don't know how good I am, but I do know that I'm always armed with hand sanitizer." She glanced at the sticky jar of parmesan cheese, victim to a hundred grubby kid hands, as Tyler reached for it and resisted the urge to wipe it down first. She had to draw the line somewhere.

"So where are you looking to live, anyway?" Bess asked casually.

"Are you moving here?" Abby asked, wide-eyed.

Mouth full of pizza, Tyler nodded his reply.

"You should live with us, Tyler!" Abigail burst out.

Bess felt the heat rush to her cheeks. "I don't think Tyler would like living with a mom and a three-year-old, honey."

"Why not?"

Tyler shot Bess a deliberate grin. "Yeah, why not, Bess?"

She narrowed her eyes on him. "Well, honey," she began, turning to Abby, "men like Tyler like to have some privacy."

"Why?"

Tyler saved her. "We're always hogging the bathrooms and the TV."

"Oh." The little girl nodded sagely.

"Besides, isn't Lacey still staying with you?" he asked.

Bess shook her head. "She and Mick just bought a condo in DC. He got stationed at the Pentagon after his treatment at Walter Reed was over."

"That's good." He angled his head. "How's he doing now, anyway?"

Bess felt awkward, not knowing how much to share. She was protective of her friends, and it had been a hard recovery for Mick. Even though he was now able to take a SEAL job at the Pentagon in Special Ops planning, he still wasn't quite back to his old self. "He's doing much better," she responded vaguely.

"TBI's serious. Glad they got him into the program at Walter Reed. There's actually a long wait list for it." He reached for a piece of pepperoni. "Bet Lacey's glad to be back home on the East coast for a while."

Bess grinned at the thought of her friend. "She's madly in love. Her home's wherever he is."

Tyler's smile seemed to fade slightly, though Bess wasn't sure.

"Good for them," he said.

"They sold their house in San Diego and made a great profit. So Lacey's hoping to do the same thing with the place in DC. It's got a nice view of the zoo, but it's kind of a mess inside. Nothing Lacey can't fix though. All cosmetic."

"Aunt Lacey has lions in her backyard now. I saw them," Abby chimed in.

"Not really in her backyard, honey. In the zoo across the street, remember?"

Abby ignored her. "They were sleeping. They didn't roar."

"So do you like having the house all to yourself, Abby?" Tyler asked.

Abby frowned. "I miss Aunt Lacey and Aunt Maeve. Aunt Vi, too. She promised she'd do a lemonade stand with me this summer."

"Aunt Vi?" Tyler looked at Bess.

"Lacey's sister. She lived with us for a few months. Didn't you meet her at Maeve and Jack's party last year?"

"Can't recall. There had to be a hundred people there."

"More like two hundred, but they filtered in and out through the night, so it didn't seem that bad."

"Someone new is coming to live with us," Abby volunteered.

Tyler raised his eyebrows. "Who?"

Bess shrugged. "We're not sure yet. But we've had a couple people in to see the place. I've got to get a housemate.

Maeve said she's not worried about it, but I know she is. And besides, I need to split the electric bill with someone."

"She hates kids."

Tyler looked to Bess for clarification.

"The last woman who came to look at the house," Bess explained.

"She hates kids," Abby repeated. "She said so."

"Well, I hope you showed her what the door is for," Tyler commented before turning to Abby. "She wasn't nice, Abby. Who couldn't love a kid like you?"

Abby beamed.

"How much are you asking for the room?" he asked Bess.

Bess told him the amount and bit her lip, seeing his eyes widen in response. Were they asking too much? "But it's really two rooms that would come with it. The master bedroom upstairs and the little office on the main floor."

Tyler shook his head. "You're asking way too little."

Relieved, Bess sighed. "Oh, I thought you were going to say it was too much."

"No way. For waterfront? Are you kidding me? That's dirt cheap."

"Yeah, but it comes with a catch, you know?" Bess glanced at Abby who was pulling the cheese off a slice and putting it in her mouth. "I run a pretty clean house. No overnight guests. No music with foul lyrics blasting through the place. That sort of thing."

"You need a nice Amish woman."

Bess laughed. "Exactly. Know any Amish who are looking to make their way in the big, bad world of Annapolis?"

"No. But I will keep my ears open. Fort Meade is a huge base. I might hear of someone who needs a place."

"Thanks." Bess smiled. "And let me know where you end up, okay? I might be looking for an apartment soon."

"Why? What do you mean?"

"Well, think about it. If Maeve didn't have Abby and me at that house, she could be renting the place for so much more money. Every month, I'm costing her." Frowning, she nabbed another slice of pizza from the tray. "If this keeps up, I feel like it's time for me to do the right thing and... you know." She glanced at her daughter, who was looking blissfully unaware of the conversation around her as she examined something on her pizza, no doubt ensuring it wasn't a stray piece of pepperoni.

Bess couldn't imagine leaving that house, which had been her home for nearly four years now, the only home that Abby had ever known. But if she couldn't find a housemate, she really didn't have a choice.

———

Tyler stood on the balcony, blankly staring at the parking lot of the cookie cutter apartment complex just west of Fort Meade. It looked exactly like the other two he had seen this afternoon.

"Can you keep a grill out here? Throw on some steaks?" he asked.

The leggy blonde who worked in the rental office grinned at him from the frame of the sliding glass door. "You're not supposed to. But I doubt anyone would report you," she said, glancing him up and down. "Especially if you were willing to share your meat."

Tyler laughed at the innuendo. She was a bold one, that's for sure. Funny and definitely interested. At another time he might be interested, too. Right now, though, he'd rather focus on finding an apartment or he'd be stuck living on base for the next year. Base living wasn't for him—always feeling there was some commander looking over his shoulder.

"The view's not very promising," he said skeptically.

"We don't have any two-bedrooms available that have a different view. If you could manage a one bedroom—"

"No, I definitely need two bedrooms."

"You have a roommate?" She looked curiously hopeful, and Tyler briefly wondered if an image of a threesome was floating into her mind.

He grinned. "No, just a lot of crap."

It was almost embarrassing that he had accumulated so much in his 27 years, and every year he swore he'd whittle down his haul to a more manageable size. But there was always something pulling him away from the task. Deployments, usually. With his last two jobs, he had spent more time OCONUS—outside the Continental U.S.—than CONUS.

Now with a year in a stateside military intelligence job in his immediate future, he might actually have some time to make a run to Goodwill and unload some stuff.

Glancing again at the view, a sea of economical cars with a couple BMWs thrown into the mix, he couldn't help imagining Bess's little Cape Cod overlooking the Chesapeake Bay. He had been there once last year when he was passing through town. He had called Bess to see if she and Abby wanted to meet up for lunch, but he had ended up getting an invitation to her friend Maeve's party that day instead.

The house was a little slice of heaven with a shoreline where he could launch his paddleboard easily for a quick tour of the coastline. A good dock for crabbing. He could picture popping open a Sam Adams and watching sunsets on that screened-in back porch any night when he managed to come home from work at a halfway decent hour.

Compared to this generic apartment with its cream-colored wall-to-wall carpet and the sound of someone's bass speakers pulsating through the walls, the house suddenly seemed like a pretty damn nice option.

He wondered if Bess would consider having a male housemate for a change. He'd had lots of friends who had female housemates, and only heard that they were generally clean and quiet compared to men. The only problems that ever seemed to arise were when some kind of attraction built up in the close quarters.

That wouldn't be the case with Bess, Tyler was certain. They'd known each other almost four years, and there wasn't the slightest spark between them. She was more like a sister, he thought, which made sense since her situation with Abigail had always reminded him of his own sister, so many years ago.

But living with a three-year-old as his other housemate? Was he ready for that?

Tyler stepped back into the bedroom of the apartment, with the rental associate in tow.

"There are two bathrooms," she pointed out. "And they'll paint the place before you move in." She traced her long, French-manicured hand along one of the scuffs on the wall. "Looks like it got a little messed up when the last people moved out. And then in here," she pointed out, placing her hand on his arm as though to guide him across the room, "you have a linen closet." Her eyes fell to where her hand met his arm. "You have some pretty powerful arms," she said, perking up a smile. "Do you box or something?"

"Mixed martial arts, actually," he stated, trying not to sound like he wasn't completely uninterested in her. Once he found a place, he'd have the time to focus on his social life again, and her inviting eyes might be more intriguing to him. "And PT every morning."

She bit her glossed lip. "That's right. I remember reading on your form that you're military. You're at Fort Meade?"

"Yeah. Ranger Battalion sent me up here to work in an intelligence support role."

"A Ranger…" she said, voice trailing.

And there it was. The Look. That look that he saw in women's eyes just about any time he said he was a Ranger. Something about Special Ops always made women melt.

He wandered into the second bedroom. It was a good size, and certainly big enough to hold his workout equipment. Holding his breath in anticipation, he moved to the window and frowned. More cars. Certainly not the best view for a workout, but it was pretty much par for the course for apartments around here.

Yet somehow, after hearing about a dirt cheap vacancy with a waterfront view, the sight of endless cars from his window made his stomach tie up.

At Bess's, he could roll out of bed and paddleboard every Saturday morning. Put out a hammock and wile away his Sunday. And when he had a date…well, he'd just have to head to her place if things heated up rather than to his place. He doubted that would turn a woman off, he figured, glancing at the lust-struck eyes of the rental associate leaning seductively against the wall. Women were pretty easy to come by when a guy wore a Ranger scroll on his right shoulder.

"So, are you interested?" she asked, clearly implying something other than his interest in the apartment.

"I'll keep it in mind," he said, looking back at the window with a frown.

She handed him her business card before he slipped out the door, inviting him to a party on Saturday night. Why did he bet the party was a party of two?

She wasn't what he was looking for. At least not at the moment. He'd keep the card handy in case he changed his mind.

Picking up his cell, he texted Bess. "How do you feel about a male roommate?" he wrote.

And he hit send.

He paused a moment and picked his phone up again, typing, "And I should add, I mow the grass and am good with plumbing."

Better to increase his chances. After all, it was one hell of a view.

CHAPTER 2

"*Tyler*? Are you serious?" Maeve's voice rang through the cell phone, and Bess could picture the wide grin on her face.

"Well, I like your reaction better than Lacey's. She thought I was out of my mind." Bess stood at the kitchen sink with her phone in hand, struggling to make some kind of dent in the morning dishes with her one remaining hand. She would have put the phone on speaker mode, but Abby was upstairs playing in her room. And Maeve had a tendency to let too many colorful words slip during a conversation.

"Hell, no, you're not. I couldn't have handpicked a better housemate for you. You're a lot safer there living with a guy you can trust as opposed to some random bozo. And he's certainly not going to do anything wrong with Mick and Jack looking over his shoulder."

Bess stooped to open the dishwasher. "You don't think they'll give him a hard time, do you?"

"Not if he behaves himself. When does he move in?"

Bess hesitated. "He actually already moved in last week."

"You waited this long to tell me?"

Bess sighed, loading the plates into the rack. "I wasn't

sure how you and Lacey would react. I know you both think I've had a crush on him or something."

"Yeah-huh. We might still think that."

Bending low to retrieve the detergent from underneath the sink, Bess struggled with the child safety lock on the cabinet door. "But I don't. I mean, anyone would find him attractive, of course. But the thing is, he's so out of my league he doesn't even tempt me."

"Girl, he could tempt an eighty-year-old nun."

"Better watch that talk about nuns. You're not Catholic, but your hubby is."

"Yeah, yeah. So what kind of a housemate is he?"

Shutting the dishwasher door, Bess paused thoughtfully. "Quiet, actually. Barely even here. His work hours are killer. He doesn't get home till after eight and he leaves at 4:30 for PT."

"Not much opportunity to impress him with your cooking skills."

She filled a cup with water from the tap. "I'm not trying to impress him, Maeve. Out of my league, remember? And if you don't remember, I'll email you a picture of my thunder thighs."

"Will you stop cutting yourself down like that? It gets old, Bess. Really."

"Oh, and you'll hate this. He planted a recliner in the middle of your living room."

"Ugh—no!" Maeve all but hissed. "A recliner? In my house?"

"Serves you right for taking most the furniture with you to Little Creek."

Maeve groaned. "Just tell me it doesn't have built-in cup holders."

"It doesn't." Bess grinned at the sigh of relief on the other end. "So anyway, except for the recliner, he's really the perfect housemate for us. I sleep so much better with him around."

Maeve scoffed. "Well, that actually makes me worry. A single woman living with a guy that looks like him should be seeing her estrogen levels at least double. You should be ordering a vibrator online just to get through the night."

Taking a sip of water, Bess rolled her eyes. "God, Maeve, you are so crude."

"Well, I have to get all the crudeness out of my system."

"Why?"

"Are you sitting down?"

Bess's heart rate picked up in pace. Knowing what she hoped to hear, she sat at the kitchen table. "I am now."

"The adoption went through. On Wednesday, we're picking up the kids."

From head to toe, Bess was covered in goosebumps. "Oh my God, Maeve." Tears welled up in her eyes.

"I'm a mom, twice over, and I didn't even have to get any stretch marks." Her voice crackled with emotion.

Bess laughed. Maeve had been unable to have children of her own, and Bess admired her sense of humor about it. "Did you tell Lacey yet?"

"Nope. You're the first. I'm calling her as soon as I get off the phone with you."

"You must be so excited." Bess could picture the kids' faces from the photos Maeve emailed her when she and Jack had first met them. The little girl was eight years old and her brother was three. They had been bounced around for years in the foster care system, just hoping someone would open their home to a pair of siblings.

"I'm beyond excited," Maeve said, the smile in her voice seeping through the phone. "I've already picked out the paint for their rooms and their furniture is ready. Everything won't be perfect by Wednesday, but it got finalized a lot quicker than we expected."

"Jack must be over the moon."

"You have no idea. Mom and Dad are coming up from Charleston tomorrow to help me paint the rooms. And Jack's parents are coming down to meet their new grandchildren later in the month."

Bess stood to refill her glass of water. "Abby will love this news. It will be nice that she and your boy are the same age, you know? What's his name again?"

"Marcus. And my girl is Kayla. Oh, I can't wait for you guys to meet them. We'll bring them up for Vi's wedding, of course." Lacey's sister Vi was getting married in a couple months and Bess would be a bridesmaid.

As Bess stood to refill her glass, Maeve's excited ramblings continued. But Bess suddenly couldn't hear the words. She caught the image of Tyler, standing on his paddleboard rowing, looking like a Greek god floating upon the water. Feeling the steam rising from her body, she gulped.

"Keep your shirt on" should have been one of the house rules she had laid out for him when he signed the rental agreement. Because Abby would grow up with a warped view of what men were supposed to look like with him hanging around the house looking like... *that.*

"Bess, are you still there?" Maeve's voice snapped her out of it.

"Um, yeah. Sorry. Got distracted."

"He's there, isn't he?" she said knowingly. There was no hiding anything from Maeve.

"Honestly, Maeve, if you could see what I am seeing from this kitchen window, you'd melt into a pool of liquid lust."

"I'm married now. I only melt for Jack."

"Well, you've never seen Tyler shirtless on a paddleboard."

"Oh, yum. I'm telling you, stake your claim on that muffin. Cook for him, and he'll be yours, Bess. No man alive can resist your cooking."

Bess snorted. Not a recipe she knew could make up for her expanded waistline and trunk-like legs. "Tyler goes for model types. Remember, I met his girlfriend from a few years ago. She could have been a cover girl for *Vogue*."

"And they broke up. So maybe he doesn't go for that sort of thing long-term. Make that lasagna that Jack and Mick always rave about."

Bess gave herself a shake. "Stop it. I can't think about things like that. I've got a good thing going here. I can't mess it up by making a move on him. Hell, I wouldn't even know how to make a move. It's been so long." She watched him step onto the shore and head toward the house. "Oh, no. Gotta run. He's back on land."

Maeve laughed. "Just don't get yourself hurt, okay? Or I'll come up there and beat the crap out of him."

"Language, Maeve," Bess reminded her.

"I know. Four more days. I'm talking like a sailor till then because it's rated G around here from then on out."

"Tell Jack congratulations for me, okay?" She put her dirty cup in the sink.

"Will do."

"Love you, new mama."

"Love you back."

Bess clicked her phone off and pulled herself away from the kitchen window.

Maeve was going to be a mom. It was so right, so perfect, and yet Bess felt a dull ache in her heart from how quickly time was passing by. Maeve and Jack would stay in Little Creek for another year at the last word from the Navy. How soon would it be before they moved back here and filled this house to capacity with their new family?

Even while she was thrilled for Maeve, she knew she had one year left to get her and Abby situated for this next stage in their lives.

Where would the road take her this time?

Abby bounded down the steps. "Did you see Tyler walking on the water?"

Bess smiled. "He was paddleboarding. Want to go see?"

Abby nodded enthusiastically and raced out the back door towards him. Bess watched from the back deck as Tyler showed Abby the board and how he moved the oar across the water. Abby was captivated, and he put the board on the ground so that she could stand on it. After about five minutes—the full length of Abby's attention span—Abby came flying back up the lawn to the patio.

"Did you see me, Mama? Did you see me paddleboarding?"

"I did, sunshine. You looked like a pro."

Tyler came up behind Abby and it was all Bess could do to not drool. His chest had a sheen of sweat that glistened in the afternoon sun and accentuated every perfectly shaped ripple of his abs. But it was always his forearms that distracted her the most. They were wider than most, with fists that could pack a punch, she imagined.

Years ago, a physique like that would have terrified Bess. Dan hadn't even had much of a build on him, and look at the damage he had been able to do.

Mick and Jack had fixed that perception. Either one of them could be lethal if he wanted to, but would never do anything except protect someone who was in need. From them, she had learned that some men could be trusted.

Over the years they had known each other, Tyler had proven himself to be cut from the same cloth as the husbands of her two best friends, or she never would have let him step foot in the same house as Abby.

"I better hit the shower," he said casually, clueless that image made Bess's heart stop momentarily.

"Going out tonight?" she asked innocently.

"No way. I'm beat after that week at work. All I want to do is relax."

As he started to walk away, Abby took his hand so naturally it made Bess's breath hitch.

"Do you like Italian?" Bess found herself calling out from behind them.

He turned back to her. "Who doesn't?"

"Great. I'm making lasagna tonight."

Tyler had died and gone to heaven.

He was generally a pretty easy person to please when it came to food. Enough time in the field eating MREs will do that to a man. If Bess had thrown in a frozen lasagna, he would have been happy she went to the trouble.

But this...

Teeth sinking into another bite, his head shook slowly and his eyes fell to half-mast. A succulent blend of tomatoes and ricotta seeped into his mouth. There was a slight texture. Was it zucchini? Peppers? He wasn't even sure. But the fresh basil—he recognized that by the scent—had been picked by Abby just that evening from the pots they kept alongside the back porch.

"I think I love you, Bess," he said. It was only a joke, and she laughed lightly in response, the tiniest hint of a blush creeping up her cheeks.

After this many years, he knew Bess well enough to know she'd never take it the wrong way. It was like that with her. She was one of those women who didn't seem to have some kind of ulterior motives in anything she did. There were no pretenses about her. She was just as straightforward and reliable as a person could get.

And natural, he couldn't help thinking, glancing at her. Not flashy at all, she could walk into a bar and never get noticed.

What a loss for the men who overlooked her, he thought as he took another bite. He knew guys who would propose to a woman after a meal like this. It was just that delicious.

She waved her hands dismissively. "Oh, it's just lasagna. Anyone can make lasagna."

"No. It takes talent to make something like this." He found himself talking with his mouth full. It was hard not to. He simply couldn't stop putting more food in his mouth.

"I'm done," Abby exclaimed, immediately crawling out of her booster seat.

Amused, Tyler looked at her plate. She had diligently removed every chunk of meat from her lasagna and formed it into a pile at the side that looked a bit like a brown snowman.

Bess frowned. "You barely ate anything."

"I ate noodles. Can I play with my Duplos now?"

Heaving a defeated breath, Bess gave in. "Okay. Put your plate by the sink, please."

Carelessly leaving her silverware behind, Abby toddled over to the sink with her plate and disappeared up the stairs.

Bess looked at Tyler. "It's nice to cook for someone who actually appreciates my meals," she confided. "I'll cook for you anytime."

"Abby has no clue what other kids have to eat. The only Italian food I ate at her age came from a can."

Bess laughed.

She had a nice laugh, Tyler decided. "I don't think I've ever had homemade pasta before."

"Really?" She sliced off another piece for him as he finished his first.

He really should stop. The last thing he could do is gain weight in this job if he wanted to stay in the Rangers.

But still, one more piece wouldn't kill him. He'd do extra PT tomorrow, he promised himself as she placed another chunk of oven-baked decadence onto his plate.

"Lacey and Maeve gave me the pasta maker for Christmas last year," she continued, completely unaware that her lasagna was a shade away from giving him a hard-on. "I'm still trying to get the hang of it."

"Believe me, you got the hang of it." He swallowed and looked at her. "Why aren't you working as a chef somewhere or something like that?"

Bess shrugged. "I don't have the training, for one thing. And I also need a steady paycheck and good benefits for Abby. The hours are good where I work. I can finish early and pick up Abby from day care at a decent hour. You can't get that if you're working in a restaurant."

It made sense, he figured, but still...

She had told him she worked as an office manager for a dental practice. Not exactly the kind of place where she could stretch the wings of her culinary talents. But he guessed that's what happened to single moms, thinking back to the financial struggles of his own mother when he was younger.

Bess gathered up Abby's silverware and added it to her own. "I work for a caterer sometimes on the weekends when they get overbooked. I get some of my recipes from that. Edith babysits Abby on those days."

"Edith?"

"She's sort of a family friend. She was Mick's sponsor when he went to the Academy years ago, and she's kind of adopted us, for some reason."

"You mean Mrs. B?"

"Yeah. That's right. Did you meet her at Maeve's party last year?"

Tyler smiled. "Yeah, I saw her then, but I met her a long time before that. She hosted a crab feast for the West Point exchange cadets when I was here a few years back. She's an incredible lady. So she babysits for Abby?"

"More than that. Treats her like a doting grandmother. Not sure what I'd do without her. With what babysitters charge, I'd never be able to do the catering job without her just because I'd barely break even."

"Well, if she's ever not available, I can watch her," Tyler said, making a mental note to pick up a spare car seat for Abby so that he could take her in his car if the need ever arose. Never hurt to be prepared, deployments overseas had taught him.

Bess dropped her gaze. "You'll have better things to do on Saturday nights than chase after a three-year-old after you get settled in your job."

Tyler thought back to the two phone messages from women he had already met here. Yeah, he could be busy any night he wanted, but right now the promise of a few hours babysitting seemed a small price to pay for a meal like this.

Give him another week or so, and he'd probably change his mind. A guy's got needs.

He scooped up another bite before taking his plate to the sink. "Any chance this caterer thing might turn into something more regular?"

"I doubt it. The only reason they hired me is they were trying to get a friend of mine to sign on with them for her wedding this fall. Vi said she'd go with someone else if they didn't hire me part-time. And seeing as her wedding's going to get a lot of press coverage, they figured it would be a good deal for them."

"Oh, yeah. She's on CNN or CNBC or one of those financial networks, isn't she?"

"Sometimes," Bess answered. "Not as regularly as she used to be, though. She's a partner in a financial firm now. She's marrying Joe Shey."

"The SEAL CO? Wow. Both sisters fell for SEALs." He chuckled softly.

"They're easy to fall for, I guess."

Tyler shrugged. SEALs got a lot more press than Rangers did, but the risks were no different. "Thanks for dinner. I owe you."

"Anytime," she said, rising from her chair.

He blocked her as she headed toward the sink. "No way. You cook. I clean up afterward. Least I can do."

For a moment, she looked like she might put up a fight about it. She had a bit of fire in her eyes, to match her red hair. But then she sat down again at the table. "It's a deal. But don't be surprised if I cook for you more often then."

Turning her chair slightly, she stretched out her legs. She looked exhausted, he thought, and there was always a hint of worry in her eyes. Maybe that came with motherhood. "Do you want a beer? I'm having one."

"No. I never drink anymore."

"Why not?" *Shit.* He cursed himself for asking. Maybe she was recovering from an addiction. *Way to go, idiot.*

"Being alone with a daughter does that to me. I just worry that something will happen and I won't be able to respond as quickly because I had a drink. What if she needs me to drive her to the ER or something? It's just me, being a control freak. I'm a bit of a paranoid mom."

"You're not paranoid. But I'm here. You can pass a little of the control to me. I never drink enough that I can't drive sober to base. With the Rangers, I was on one-hour recall. If I needed to deploy, I had to be ready. The enemy won't wait for us to sober up. So, do you want a beer? Truth."

Pausing, she looked as though there was a debate brewing inside of her. Finally she answered, "I'm not really a beer drinker. But a glass of wine sounds divine right now."

"Then I'm getting you a glass of wine. If Abby needs to make a run to the ER, God forbid, I'm ready. Where do you keep the wine?"

Bess glanced upward. "I think Maeve left some in the cabinet above the fridge."

He reached up for a bottle and glanced at the label. He knew little to nothing about wine. White or red. That was it. "Chardonnay," he read. "Sound up your alley?"

"Sounds perfect."

He felt her eyes follow him as he searched for the corkscrew in the silverware drawer.

"One hour recall," she said thoughtfully. "Sounds a little like motherhood. But I don't get to drive a tank."

Stabbing the cork and twisting, Tyler laughed. "Recall is one thing I don't miss about being down there."

"But the rest you miss?"

"Yeah. I've wanted to be a Ranger since I was a kid. Even though I'm still working on their behalf up here for the year, I'd rather be in the action. There's not a lot of years you can do this, you know."

"What do you mean?"

"Oh, you get banged up pretty bad, even in the best of circumstances. Even in training, I've known guys to get serious injuries. I'm 27, and I've already got two compressed discs in my back from the Infantry lifestyle. And this," he said, kicking his one foot against his other calf as he poured a glass of wine.

"What?"

"This. Got a good chunk of flesh blown off me in my last

mission." He pointed to a long, jagged scar on his calf camou-flaged by the ripples of muscles and the hairs on his leg. "Half the reason they sent me here rather than someone else is because my leg needed more time to heal. I'm much more of a field guy than MI."

"MI?"

"Sorry. Military Intelligence." He laughed. "Though there are those who will tell you that's an oxymoron."

Bess shook her head, eyes fixed on the scar. "I don't know why you do it."

Tyler set the glass in front of her. "Ahhh. Then you weren't paying attention in your freshman history class."

"Huh?"

"That was the year we studied World War II in high school—the first time I heard about Ranger Battalion. They were the ones who led the charge onto Omaha Beach to establish a foothold, retake France, and defeat the Nazis. We saw a documentary on it, and it blew my mind. The footage was phenomenal. We saw these guys storming the beach, climbing ropes to get up those cliffs, doing whatever it took to make it. If they had turned back, we might be speaking German right now." He sat back down at the table. "I wanted to be a part of that fighting force. That history. That's where the motto comes from, you know. 'Rangers lead the way.' It dates back to Omaha Beach."

"I never knew that," she said softly. "I'm not too up on the whole Special Operations thing." A soft laugh escaped her.

"What?"

Amused at something, she shook her head. "When we first met back when I was pregnant, and you said you wanted to be a Ranger, I thought you meant Park Ranger."

Tyler tossed back his head, laughing. "That's just classic."

"Yeah. I asked Mick later why you were going to West

Point if you wanted to eventually become a Park Ranger and he never lets me forget it. He still brings it up."

Tyler was still chuckling. "Well, you're the first then. Down in Savannah all the girls know who the Rangers are. In the St. Paddy's Day Parade, we march in formation at the front of the parade, and they jump into the street to kiss us. By the end of the parade, we've got lipstick all over our faces."

"You're exaggerating."

"Not one bit. I have pictures for proof."

She took a sip of wine. "So is that why you went to West Point? So you could become a Ranger?"

"No, that's why I enlisted."

Bess paused. "Enlisted? I don't get it. You're an officer."

"I enlisted in the Army right out of high school. Got a couple deployments under my belt. Then one of my commanders, a West Point grad, suggested I try to get in. He walked me through the process, wrote a recommendation, and suddenly, I'm on the road to being an officer."

Bess took another sip from her glass, and Tyler noticed how her eyelids half shut as she did, as though in intense appreciation of the drink. Yep, it had definitely been a while since she'd had any alcohol. Not very typical for a 24-year old, he thought, his mind wandering to his recent dates who all seemed to be addicted to the party scene.

She should be out, having fun with her friends, like other girls her age.

Instead, she was working two jobs, ignoring her talents so that she could provide for her daughter, and getting buzzed off one glass of chardonnay with a guy who was more like a brother to her than anything else.

He couldn't help feeling sorry for her, even though he knew she'd hate that.

"I really meant what I said, Bess. About babysitting," he

heard himself say. He nearly cringed, knowing that if she took him up on it too regularly, his sex life could only go south. But this was Bess. She wasn't the type to take advantage.

"Oh, thanks. But Edith really loves being around Abby any chance she gets."

"But you should get out more. You should—" he paused, gathering the daring to step on a hornet's nest, "—date. You know? You're 24. You need more fun in your life."

Bess shrank slightly in her chair and he immediately regretted saying it.

"I do date sometimes," she countered, and from the uneasiness of her tone, he knew it wasn't true. A woman like Bess didn't lie easily, even to save face.

"I'm sure you do," he said quickly. "But I'm just saying if you need a little more fun in your life, may as well get it now, while I'm living here and available."

Eyes widening, she gave him the strangest look. An odd mix of amusement and disbelief, as if she had some inside joke she almost wanted to share. Almost, but not quite, because all she chose to say was, "Thanks, Tyler. I'll keep that in mind."

CHAPTER 3

"If you need a little more fun in your life, may as well get it now *while I'm living here and available?*" Lacey repeated in between peals of laughter. Her hands dangerously covered in paint, she doubled over onto her bed in hysterics. "Does he seriously not know how that would sound to you?"

Bess pulled her paint roller from the wall to glance over her shoulder at her friend. "No clue whatsoever. I think he sees me as a little sister or something, and just assumes that I think he's my adopted big brother."

"If only he knew." Lacey blew a lock of hair from her eyes as she stood up from the bed. Even speckled with beige paint and dressed in her most utilitarian painting clothes, she looked so much better than she had in ages. The past year had been hard on her, but now that Mick had returned to duty, the light had come back into her eyes.

"Yeah, no kidding. If I had a second glass of wine, I might have stripped my clothes off and told him just what kind of fun I needed right now." Bess poured more paint from the can into the roller tray. They were only half finished painting Lacey and Mick's bedroom and almost out of paint. Who would have known it would take three coats to cover the oxblood red walls favored by the condo's previous owner?

"Is he still gone most the time?" Lacey asked.

An ache building in her hand, Bess set down her roller and stretched her fingers. "He's at the house more now than he was at first. Always seems to make it home in time for dinner."

"What man wouldn't after he's sampled your cooking? I think Mick still wants to move back in with you. Those months when we were trying to settle on a condo he got spoiled with you making him dinner every night."

Sighing, Bess leaned against the bed. "I don't know, Lacey. Seeing Tyler walk in the door in his uniform every day? Looking like a total 'muffin,' as Maeve would say. It's starting to kind of get to me."

Lacey eyed her friend. "Don't say I didn't warn you."

Bess rolled her eyes dramatically. "You were right. I was wrong. Do you want me to put it in writing?"

In triumph, Lacey gave a smirk before she resumed painting. "Well, does having him around at least make you feel better about the Dan problem?"

Bess gave a careless wave of her hand, nearly dripping paint on the floor as she did. "Oh, yeah. Completely. I haven't thought I've seen Dan since that time in the car."

"Good. It was probably just nerves, you know. After four years, I really doubt you'd even recognize him. And it's hard living by yourself in your situation, especially with your history. The wounds that are the hardest to heal are the ones you can't see. That's what Mick really learned this past year."

"How's he doing?" Bess lifted the glass of lemonade that rested on Lacey's dresser. "I mean, he looks great. But what's going on inside, you know?"

Frowning, Lacey tossed her head to the side. "He still struggles. His hands shake sometimes, and for a guy who used to be able to change a magazine in an HK416 in under a second, it's really knocked his ego down a couple notches."

"How's his memory?"

Lacey raised her brow. "Well, I promise he won't forget to bring Abby home from the zoo in time for lunch."

Bess wasn't worried about such a thing. Mick would never take a risk when it came to Abigail. "I know that. I mean, just overall—at work and stuff?"

"He writes a lot of lists to keep track of things, like his therapist told him to. He always comes home from work with fifteen notes he wrote on the back of his hand in pen. I tell him he should write it all on a sheet of paper, but then he laughs and tells me he'd forget where he left the paper." She smiled. "But he must be doing all right because they're loving him at the Pentagon. It's not often they get a SEAL with as much field experience in these planning jobs." Pulling her roller off the wall, she paused briefly to look out the window at the entrance to the National Zoo across the street. "It's not the same for him, though."

"I can imagine." Bess wiped off a drip of paint that had fallen onto the hardwood floor.

"He always told me he'd be fine if I told him I needed him to give up the risky stuff. But it's different when the decision was made *for* him, rather than *by* him."

"I don't think anyone would like that." Bess could somehow relate to that in the smallest sense, though she'd never admit it, even to her best friends. Being a single mom tended to make her decisions for her. Instead of going to culinary school, or even just working in a restaurant kitchen full-time, she was sitting in an office chair, with the sound of a dentist's drill providing background noise forty hours a week.

But, how she loved her little girl! And if this job provided stability and benefits, then Bess would gladly postpone her own dreams for the next fifteen or so years till Abby was ready to live on her own.

Lacey rested her hands on her hips, stepping back from her work. As her friend cocked a critical eye at the wall, Bess braced herself. Lacey was notorious for changing her mind about paint colors.

"What?" Bess dared to ask.

"I hope I chose the right color. Doesn't it look a little pinkish to you?"

Bess answered quickly. "It's cream. There's no pink in there."

Pressing her lips together, Lacey glowered at the wall. "Maybe it's just the lighting. Mick would have a fit if he had to sleep in a pink bedroom."

Bess laughed. "Well, Maeve will have a fit when she hears you painted it cream and not something a little more daring." Maeve was an interior designer who often said hell for her would be a beige house.

"I know. But if I want to turn around and sell this place in a year, I want to keep it pretty neutral." Lacey set down her roller and massaged her wrist. "Let's take a break, huh?"

"You'll get no complaint from me." Bess put her roller in the pan and went to the kitchen sink to wash her hands, with Lacey following behind her. "I thought it would be easier to paint than pushing Abby's stroller all over the zoo today. But I'm thinking we got the bad end of the deal."

"No kidding."

"I just hope Abby sees that lion roar. It's all she talks about. She's obsessed with lions."

Lacey frowned. "Won't happen. All it does is sleep during the day. But sometimes when we leave the windows open at night we can hear it first thing in the morning."

"Really?" Crossing the room, Bess glanced out the living room window briefly at the view of the zoo. A prime location in Washington, DC, Lacey's Connecticut Avenue address was impressive, and the deal she had struck with the seller was even better. Her eyes wandered to the new granite countertop in the kitchen and built-in shelves framing the gas fireplace. Already, the condo was looking like a showpiece. "I don't know why you'd want to sell this place after you've put so much work into it. It's gorgeous now."

"Not quite. But it's getting there. We should make a nice profit on it since we got it for such a low price."

"You're sounding more and more like your sister every day."

"I do get to see her more now that we're living in the same city. So maybe she's rubbing off on me." Lacey laughed. "But really, it's time for us to be living in a house, not a condo. Something with a yard. And good schools."

"Schools?" Bess said warily.

"Yep." Lacey sent her a smile. "We've decided we want to start trying to have a baby."

"Oh, Lacey, that's wonderful."

"I hope so. I really do."

Bess's brow creased. "How could it not be?"

"I don't know. It's been such a hard year, you know? We just couldn't even think about having a newborn around when Mick was still recovering. But things are as normal as they're ever going to be now. I guess it's time."

"Another friend for Abby. With just three years difference, they'll probably want to play together at some point."

"Four years difference at least," Lacey corrected. "I'm not pregnant yet."

"Everything changes so quickly, doesn't it? Maeve's a mom now, and you're headed that way. Vi will probably be next. Can you just see her bouncing around a baby?"

Lacey scoffed. "Actually, no. I really doubt she and Joe will have kids. Vi's never expressed much interest, and I think Joe's on the same page."

"I know. But after they get married this fall, those baby-making hormones might kick in yet. You never know."

Lacey smiled, walking into the kitchen. "Did you pick up your bridesmaid dress yet?"

Bess nodded glumly, following her in and pulling out a counter stool. "It's hanging in my closet, but I haven't put it on yet. I hope I didn't gain weight again."

"I hope not too, because Vi will kill you."

Bess noted that there wasn't much sarcasm in Lacey's tone. Vi was so stressed about her upcoming wedding. At first, they had thought they'd do something small. But when Joe managed to snag the U.S. Naval Academy Chapel for the service, the guest list started to explode. "It'll fit. If I have to sweat off ten pounds of water in a sauna the morning of the wedding, that's what I'll do."

"You'll be fine," Lacey assured her. "Did you see her talking on CNN about hedge funds last week? The guy who was interviewing her actually asked about her wedding. She played it off, but looked totally annoyed with the guy. I mean, what does her wedding have to do with hedge funds? There will probably be lots of press there."

"So long as they're taking pictures of Vi and Joe and not my lard ass in a chiffon dress."

"Bess, stop talking about yourself like that," Lacey scolded as she handed her a Diet Coke. "We're all sick of it. Is that how you want Abby to think of you? As a lard ass?"

Slumping slightly, Bess opened the can. "I know. And I don't say those things in front of her. But since becoming a mom, my weight only seems to move in one direction. Up."

"Kids are smart," Lacey continued. "They pick up on things. If you started wearing something other than ratty old t-shirts, maybe you'd feel better about yourself. I mean, Bess, there's a hole in that t-shirt." Lacey eyed the lower portion of Bess's shirt. "It belongs in the trash."

"It's a good painting t-shirt. Besides, it's a tiny hole. No one can see." Bess narrowed her eyes on Lacey.

"We all know your rule for holes in your clothes, Bess. You won't throw it away unless a fist can fit through it. Now that Tyler's living with you—"

"We're just friends, Lacey. Housemates. I'm not getting a new wardrobe just because I've got a man in the house, okay? Now lay off me or I won't help you re-paint your damn room when Mick comes home and tells you it's pink."

Laughing, Lacey raised her hands up in surrender. "Okay, okay."

It was nearly midnight, a respectable hour to come home after a date. But in reality, the hours spent with Kristina, an aesthetician he had met while filling up at the gas station, had been more painful than Ranger School.

He stepped through the door, quickly punching the code into the security system. He didn't know why they bothered with the expense of a security system in this safe of a neighborhood. But if he had a kid himself, then he'd probably be just as cautious.

The house was silent, except for the hardwood creaking beneath his feet as he padded across the kitchen. The sight of Bess and Abby asleep in his recliner in the living room caught his eye.

Abby probably had fallen asleep first, he imagined, and Bess right after. It was Saturday, so Bess had likely been working her second job that night, and was too tired to even make it up the stairs with Abby.

The woman worked too damn hard.

Cautiously, Tyler stepped toward them and rested his hand against the bottom of Abby's pants. The diaper was still dry, he could tell. Abby was struggling with potty training, and most nights she pretty much floated out of bed if she didn't wear a diaper.

He pulled the throw blanket from the sofa and placed it gently over them both.

Watching them for a moment, both in a peaceful slumber, Tyler was struck by their similarities. Abby looked so much like her mother that he had to remind himself that half of Abby's genes came from someone else.

Tyler never asked about him. Why would he? The guy, whoever he was, obviously wasn't a father. It took action, not just a genetic donation, to make a guy a father. Sleepless nights rocking a colicky baby. Wrinkles of worry each time cold and flu season crept into the house. Frantic doctor appointments when a child didn't meet a milestone on time.

So the guy who donated 50% of Abby's chromosomes was as much of a dad as Tyler's own father had been. As useless as tits on a bull.

It was no wonder Tyler felt a kinship with the little girl. He had been lucky in the same way Abby was; he had been gifted with a mother who would do anything for him, even if she had to do it alone.

Bess sighed in her sleep, her grasp on her daughter tightening slightly. Bess's red curls framed her face and even though those gorgeous blue eyes of hers were closed, she looked almost angelic. She was…

…pretty. The realization of it shouldn't have surprised him. He had always thought Bess was kind of cute. But since he thought of her as a sort of honorary sister, he didn't dare look too closely.

Yet somehow, after an evening with his date, with her harsh makeup, dense eye shadow, and disparaging comments for every other woman within a hundred foot radius, Bess looked so wholesomely beautiful to him right now that it almost caused a little ache inside his gut.

Which must mean he was hungry, of course. Kristina had wanted to go for sushi. But the problem with sushi is that no matter how much he ate, he was always hungry thirty minutes later.

He stepped away from Bess and Abby. Probably a good thing to do anyway, because if he started thinking of Bess as being any kind of "pretty," he might end up with an awkward year lease ahead of him.

CHAPTER 4

Nearly three weeks had passed since Bess thought she'd seen Dan behind the wheel of the red Lotus. She hoped that having Tyler living with her had somehow tamed her paranoia.

So it was more of a jolt to her system that night when she passed her bedroom window and spotted the same car parked across the street. Quickly, she flicked off her light so no one would see her from outside and peered out her window for a better look.

The car's lights were out. It wasn't running. Probably just someone visiting the neighbor.

Grabbing her robe, she headed downstairs for a better look. The house was dark, and Bess could hear Abigail's soft breathing coming from her room. Tiptoeing down the steps, she passed Tyler's closed door.

With the living room lights off, she went for a closer look from the window of the small room where Tyler had set up his workout equipment. From there, she might be able to see the license plate number, or at least be able to tell whether they were Pennsylvania tags.

By the time she made it to the window, the car was gone. Bess stood there, eerily wondering if it was all in her imagination. It was late, and God knows she was tired.

But that wasn't it. Couldn't be. She *had* seen a red Lotus. Or at least it looked red. The street was pitch black out. And had it really been a Lotus? She had never been too good at identifying makes of cars. But it was pretty hard to mistake a Lotus.

Biting her lip, she leaned against the window and looked at the small room filled with Tyler's workout equipment—a treadmill that looked like it had seen more than a few miles of use, a speed bag, some weights, and a large, cylindrical heavy bag that hung from a steel stand.

A punching bag. She touched it with a sympathetic smile. *I know just how you feel.* She had been struck, felt that crack of a fist against her cheekbone, heard the crunching sound as her teeth clattered in her mouth.

What would it feel like to hit back?

Her hand on the bag, she could feel the smooth texture of the dark, aged leather. Curious, she gathered her fingers into a fist and hit it. Just a little. Pain rang out from her hand up to her shoulder.

God, she was weak.

She stood back a couple feet from the bag and punched again. Her hand ached from the impact and she let out a small curse.

"You might want to put on gloves when you do that."

Tyler's voice made her jump at least two inches in her bare feet. With PT shorts slung low on his hips, his bare upper body filled the doorway. She felt trapped somehow, frightened, probably still reeling from the thoughts of Dan that she had let slip into her consciousness.

This was Tyler, not Dan, she reminded herself.

"You scared me. I thought you were asleep," she finally

said, stepping back from the bag, nearly tripping on a free weight in the process.

"Whoa," he said as he held his arm out to steady her.

His simple touch usually quickened her heartbeat, but this time it slowed it back to its normal pace, as though her body knew that—red Lotus or not—all would be well with Tyler here.

"Sorry," she said. "I should have asked before using your stuff."

"You can use it anytime you want." Reaching behind him, he grabbed some gloves that hung on a hook. "But put these on first. You can do some damage to your hands without them. Here." Pulling her hand toward him, he gently slipped one glove on her, and then the other. The gesture of him dressing her—even if it was with boxing gloves—made her insides hum.

"This time, when you punch it, bend at the knees and the waist a little so the impact doesn't jolt your body." He stood behind her and put his hands on her waist, setting free a surge of butterflies in her stomach. "Like this. Now when you hit someone, you need to lean into him. Let the force not just come from your arm, but from your whole body."

Bess hit the bag again. This time, the pain was in her shoulder, but as she saw the bag move slightly from the impact, she felt a hint of satisfaction.

"Good. Again."

She struck it, this time following a right punch with a second one from her left hand.

"How's that feel?"

Bess cracked a grin. "Actually really good."

Tyler smiled back. "There's something kind of gratifying about beating the crap out of something, isn't there?"

The smile on Bess's face vanished, the words somehow striking her differently from how he intended them. She had once been the punching bag at the end of a rough day. She turned back to the bag, hoping he didn't notice her sudden frown.

"What women should always learn to do is kick, though," he continued.

"Kick?"

"Your strongest muscles are in your legs. If some guy is attacking you, kicking can be more effective than punching. Kick him in the balls. Just don't practice it on me, okay?"

She laughed.

"And if you are going to punch, go for the Adam's apple. Poke his eyes out. And scream like hell. Women don't scream enough. Girls grow up being told to keep quiet. It starts to become part of them. You should never lose the ability to scream." Cringing, he let out a low snicker. "Sorry. Can you tell I've given this lecture to my sister once or twice over the years? I'll be hell to have around when Abby gets to be a little older. I'll turn her into Ronda Rousey."

Bess couldn't help feeling gratified by the idea that he'd still be around then. "Who's Ronda Rousey?" she asked, eyeing the bag again.

"Best female fighter out there, in my opinion. Now, attack that bag, champ."

Bess pictured Dan's face eye-level on the bag. She punched it first, then kicked. The first kick was timid, just to see what it would feel like. The second, more powerful, once in imaginary Dan's groin, and once in the ribs, for old time's sake, remembering the time he had kicked her in the ribs on the bathroom floor. "How's that feel, asshole?" A voice inside her demanded, and then she blushed when she realized she had said it out loud.

Tyler laughed. "I think the bag would say you pack a hell of a kick."

Mortified, Bess took off the gloves. "Sorry. Got a little too carried away. I'll have to only do this when Abby's asleep, huh?"

"Keep going. It's good for you. If you want to build those leg muscles some more, try the treadmill and put it on incline. Just don't push it too hard. I know CPR, but I'd like to avoid needing to use it on you."

Fighting the blush that was creeping up her neck, she tried to erase from her mind the titillating image of Tyler giving her mouth-to-mouth. She pulled the gloves off. "Thanks. I might give it a try."

"Good. Nothing better for Abigail than having a strong mama."

Her brow furrowed and she quickly looked away. "I am a strong mama," she muttered, stalking quickly out of the room. *Great, another man who thinks I'm a weak victim. Just what I needed.*

He grabbed her arm to stop her. "Wait, Bess. I didn't mean it that way. You are strong. You're right. You're raising your kid on your own. You're more determined and selfless than any 24-year old I've ever known."

Bess cursed the tears welling in her eyes.

"Hey," he said softly, brushing a stray tear from cheek. "You are strong," he said again. "You're a survivor."

How did he know that? How had he figured that out without even knowing what she had survived?

With his finger, he lifted her chin a little. "I'm just overly protective. First time I got into a fight at school, it was over my sister, you know."

"Your sister was younger than you?" Bess asked.

"Older, actually. She got pregnant in high school. Some kid in my kindergarten class made some comment about it and they couldn't pull me off him fast enough. It pretty much stayed that way till I graduated from high school."

Curious, Bess cocked her head to the side. "Did she keep the baby?"

"Oh, yeah. Mom pretty much raised my niece like her own so that my sister could stay in school, and get her college degree. My mom's strong like you. Nothing stops her from making sure her kids have a good life."

Bess sank into the sofa. "Is that why you're so good with Abby? You're used to having a little kid in the house."

With a careless shrug, he sat beside her. "Abby's a great kid. It's easy to have her around. But yeah, having a kid around doesn't exactly seem foreign to me."

A realization struck Bess. "That's why you stayed with me in the hospital that day when Abby was born. Even after Lacey and Maeve showed up. You stayed all through my labor. I reminded you of your sister."

"Maybe. Don't know really. It just seemed the right thing to do."

It all made so much more sense to her. Tyler treated Abby and her so well because he felt sorry for them. If it had been anyone else, Bess would have felt insulted, or at the very least, defensive. But for some reason, it didn't bother her with him. She glanced his way. "You're right, you know."

"About what? I'm right so seldom, I want to mark this day in my calendar."

Bess smiled. "I do need to get stronger. I've gotten so out of shape since I was pregnant. I've embraced motherhood, one fat fold at a time."

Shaking his head, Tyler frowned. "Don't say that. You look like a woman. I won't let you step foot in that room again if your ambition is to look like some photoshopped model who has the hips of a ten-year-old boy. But if you want to get strong—that I'll get behind."

Bess glanced at the room with its intimidating equipment, and felt the strange urge to conquer it, even if she might need to ask for a defibrillator for her next birthday.

"You know," Tyler began, standing up, "if you ever want to go to the gym with me in the evenings, you're welcome to. I can get you a few visitor passes to try it out. There's even a child care room Abby would probably love."

"Isn't it on base? I can't go there without a military ID."

"Not that one. I show up there at zero-five-hundred in the morning. I don't think you'd be interested in that."

"No doubt."

"Some evenings and Saturday mornings, I go to an MMA gym off base. You know, mixed martial arts. Brazilian jujitsu. Grappling. Cage fights. That sort of thing. They've got some women's classes, too. Something to think about."

Bess cracked a smile at the thought of herself in a mixed martial arts gym trying to take down an opponent the way she had seen in the fights Tyler would watch on TV after Abby had gone to bed.

Bess Foster. In a cage fight.

Nope. Not in this lifetime.

CHAPTER 5

Bess loved Saturday mornings. There was no racing to get ready for work and rush Abby off to day care which, now that it was September, was referred to as "preschool" as some kind of justification to charge more.

Tyler, a creature of habit, always spent the morning at the gym or out on his paddleboard till at least nine o'clock. This meant Bess could hang out around the house braless in her rattiest old t-shirt and pajama shorts without feeling the slightest hint of shame or modesty.

Waking up at six, Bess had at least an hour of peace until Abby woke up. Eyeing the kitchen that awaited her as she opened the living room shades to the morning light, she wondered what recipe she'd pick out today. Something that involved a little more prep time, as always. Saturday mornings were perfect for baking, the extra minutes of freedom spent kneading and watching dough rise. She never had time for that on weekdays.

Pinwheel rolls. That's what she'd make this morning. Abby's favorite breakfast treat—the kind that oozed out cinnamon and butter, and were glazed with white frosting that dribbled over the edges. Tyler would love a few of those when he came home from his workout.

His workout, she thought, her eyes drifting to the room with the equipment that she hadn't dared to touch since that night she thought she had seen Dan.

She really should try out that treadmill some day. Work out the muscles that were atrophying in her legs. Chasing after a three-year-old was exhausting, but probably not the kind of exercise her body desperately needed. There was just never enough free time.

She hmmphed to herself. *Free time.* Time was exactly what she had now, yet how was she planning on spending it? Dipping her finger into the bowl as she concocted another Saturday morning sinful confection.

Tyler was right. Abby needed a strong mama, certainly more than she needed a dozen pinwheel rolls this morning. Apprehensively, Bess stepped into the room, the cumbersome equipment somehow mocking her.

Come on in, Bess, it seemed to beckon. *You won't last long in here.*

Narrowing her eyes, she turned on her heel and headed up to get her running shoes. They weren't the fanciest kind, certainly not what a real runner would wear. But they'd likely do well enough for whatever speed she could manage to muster.

Shoes on, she strode back down the stairs on a mission, staring down the intimidating room as she approached. Anyone else, she imagined, would have real workout clothes to wear. But all by herself, her t-shirt and frayed pajama shorts would do just fine. She had no one to impress here.

She stepped onto the treadmill and gazed at all the buttons, feeling hopeful at the sight of one labeled, "Quick Start."

She pressed it, and it began to move. Slowly—too slowly even for her out-of-shape self. What was a good running speed for a beginner? Shrugging, she punched up the speed to five miles per hour, and it slowly sped up. And sped up more, until her legs were striding along at a comparable pace to what she'd seen from joggers in the street. She wouldn't win any 5K at this speed, but it was respectable.

Yet her legs were struggling to keep up. Feet pounding, she wobbled. Was she supposed to run flat-footed, or up on the balls of her feet the way she always chased Abby when she was running astray?

As the arches of her feet fired off pain, she answered her own question, switching to a flat-footed run. She pounded onward, feeling the jarring in her knees. Everything soft on her body, which was pretty much *everything* on her body, bounced.

Suddenly she understood why women invested in good jogging bras. Even if she had her normal bra on, it probably wouldn't have given her the support she needed right now.

Trying not to glance down at the elapsed time, her lungs actually ached. Thirty seconds. Sixty seconds. And *oh dear Lord*, only ninety seconds and she was already heaving, tapping furiously at the button that reduced her speed till she found herself walking at a more manageable 3.5 miles per hour. Her eyes caught a glimpse of the warning label affixed to the machine. *Contact your doctor before beginning any exercise regimen, indeed.*

Ninety seconds? She could only run ninety seconds? That was pathetic. What if there was an emergency? What if Abby was in some kind of trouble and the only way to get to her was to run? She'd collapse by the time she made it to the end of her block.

Seriously, this just wouldn't do.

She stopped the treadmill and raced upstairs to get her

iPod. About 55 minutes till Abby woke up. And if she was going to spend it torturing herself getting stronger, she might as well do it listening to Lady Gaga.

Pulling into the driveway, Tyler's back seized up even putting the damn car into park. He was too young to start having back problems, but his last mission had caused a little more damage than he cared to admit. It wasn't enough to send him to seek a medical profile, and thank God for that, because the Rangers would have no place for him. But it did make grappling on the mats with the guys a helluva lot more difficult some mornings, especially when he was trying to get out of a rear naked choke.

Feeling like an old man, Tyler had finished up early, deciding to spend the rest of the morning on his back, hopefully with one of those baked goods that Bess always seemed to create on Saturdays.

From the lack of chaos that met him at the door, Tyler figured Abby must still be sleeping. He had no idea what time everyone got up in this house on Saturday mornings, having always spent this part of the weekend in the gym or paddle-boarding on the Bay. He sniffed the air, an unconscious action since living here, to see what Bess was making in the kitchen. But there was... nothing. Nothing except the sound of feet pounding and the whirring hum of his treadmill.

Stepping further into the house to investigate, he saw Bess walking at a fast pace on the treadmill, her stubby red ponytail bobbing behind her as she apparently rocked out to something on her iPod. With her back to him, she hadn't noticed him walk in, and he wasn't going to disturb her. Poor woman didn't get much time to herself and he wasn't about to stop her from working out.

Good for her, he thought, feeling a swell of pride.

Stepping into the kitchen, he noticed a definite lack of baked goods awaiting him on the counter. Damn, he was getting spoiled with all her good home cooking. Last week, she had even packed up leftovers for him for lunch in little plastic containers. They sure tasted better than the cafeteria food he generally picked up mid-day. Although the guys at work all seemed to think he was married. After all, what single man on the planet gets to enjoy leftover beef bourguignon for lunch?

He had hit the lottery of housemates when he had moved in with Bess.

He really should do something for her—for them. Take them to Pirate Pop's again or maybe one of those touristy cruises on the Bay. A memory struck him of a sign on base reminding Troops about the Twilight Tattoo coming up at Fort Meade. Abby would love that. The Army band would be playing, and the Drill Team from the Old Guard was a hell of a sight.

It was a big family event, not something he'd normally go to, but Tyler could picture Abby dancing around on the lawn of the parade field to the tune of *Stars and Stripes Forever.*

Drinking a glass of water from the tap, he was staring out the kitchen window at the view of the Chesapeake wondering if his back would hold up to a little paddleboarding this morning, when he heard the treadmill stop behind him. A heave of relief came from the other room, and it made Tyler grin. The first workout was always the hardest.

The light padding of footsteps approached and he turned around—

Holy shit!

A shocked look on her face, Bess stood framed in the doorway of the kitchen, obviously not expecting company.

59

But the expression on her face was probably nothing compared to his own.

Eyes up, asshole. Eyes up.

A threadbare white t-shirt, drenched in sweat, clung to her like she was the headliner in a wet t-shirt contest. And *damn*, Bess would win hands down.

"Hey," she said, surprise in her voice, and not the least attempt to cover what was right now making Tyler feel horny as a three-balled tomcat. She had no clue she was as good as naked right now, waist up. "You're home early."

"Yeah," he said, his voice quavering a little, so he took another sip of water. "Sorry if I surprised you." If he stood in the room much longer, he'd have to throw the water over his head just to cool down.

Bess had a rack. A prize-winning stunner of a rack. Tits as full and tempting as in a twelve-year-old boy's wet dream.

Which, of course, was a completely inappropriate thought to have about someone he had always considered something like a sister to him. What the hell was the matter with him? It's not like he hadn't seen breasts before on a woman. And hell, these had been *working* breasts, mom boobs, not the kind a guy was supposed to fantasize about at all.

Get it together, horn dog. "You enjoy the treadmill?" he asked, quickly turning his back to refill his quarter-empty glass, more out of respect than out of need.

"Yeah. Shocker, isn't it? I loved it."

Not even looking at her, he could tell there was a smile in her voice.

"Felt good to actually feel my heart pumping. I don't know the last time I worked up a sweat like this."

Yeah, no kidding. That would explain why she had no clue that a thin white t-shirt wasn't the thing you work out wearing, especially braless.

Glancing briefly—very briefly—over his shoulder, he saw her pull her sweaty hair out of the ponytail. "I'm gross. I better go shower."

Tyler just nodded, devilishly tempted to ask if he could join her. Giving himself a visible shake, he stalked over to the fridge just to keep his eyes off her. "Um, hey, Bess. There's a Twilight Tattoo this week on base. You want me to take you and Abby?"

Dead silence met his invitation and he had no choice but to look at her again. Only look at her eyes, he commanded himself noticing they were as blue as the waters he used to paddleboard over when he was stationed in Schofield Barracks, Hawaii.

"Uh, I'm not really a body art kind of person." Confused, Bess's wide eyes were almost as big as what was peering at him through her t-shirt seven inches below her face. With the AC pumped up, her nipples were standing at attention, just like one particular organ on his own body was poised to do any minute.

Sister. Sister. She's like my sister.

Tyler swallowed. What exactly was proper etiquette in this kind of situation? If he told her to go cover up, she'd be mortified. But if he didn't say anything, that would make him some kind of perv. He opted to turn his back again, pretending to search for something in the refrigerator. "Not that kind of tattoo. Twilight Tattoo is a kind of military tradition that dates back to the Revolution. The U.S. Army Band comes to play. The Old Guard will be there and the Army Drill Team." He reached for a yogurt, even though he hated yogurt, and started to peel back the foil top. "I think Abby would love it," he finished, toying with the foil before tossing it in the recycle bin, back still turned.

"Oh, sounds nice. Yeah, totally sounds like something Abby would like. Thanks."

Okay, good. Now please put some dry clothes on.

Instead, she pulled a chair out from the table to sit down.

Crap. His stomach churned. He wasn't going to sit at that table staring at her tits eating yogurt he hated. "Um, were you going to shower? Because I'm gonna need to in a few minutes and I don't want to use up all the hot water."

"Oh, yeah. Sorry. Okay," she said, turning and walking out of the kitchen, seeming somewhat flustered.

Ha. *She* was flustered? How about him? He shouldn't have had such a reaction. He should have played big brother to her and laughed it off saying, "Hey, you might to cover up those headlights or the boys in the neighborhood will start swarming the place."

Instead, he found himself struggling for words—even for breath, for that matter.

Had he actually said he'd be needing a hot shower?

Cold shower. Definitely a cold shower this morning.

She couldn't blame Tyler for kicking her out of the kitchen. She must smell like a dead sewer rat. And she probably looked twice as bad.

Stepping into the bathroom, she didn't dare look into the mirror. Granted, in the first couple weeks of Tyler living with her, she had hesitated to emerge from her room without at least a little mascara and lip gloss. But over time, she started to loosen up, daring to show him her completely bare face and the worst of her old t-shirts, the ones Maeve swore she'd burn one day when she came to visit.

After all, if she were to survive the next year with him, he may as well witness what she looked like on a normal day.

But bearing the sight of her crawling off the treadmill,

covered in three coats of sweat after her first workout since high school gym class was a lot to ask of a guy.

The hot water pummeled her body and Bess grinned, feeling strangely satisfied with herself after a half hour of self-imposed torture on the treadmill.

She was going to have to do that again.

CHAPTER 6

She had totally gone overboard, she thought as she unloaded a huge plastic storage bin filled with fried chicken, a plate of lemon squares, fruit salad, and a bowl of curry chicken and grapes casserole.

It would have been more picturesque to pack a wicker picnic basket, but she didn't have one, so had to improvise.

There was enough food to feed an army which, seeing as they were sitting smack dab in the center of an Army base, could only work to her advantage.

Until today, the Naval Academy had been the only military installation she had ever stepped foot upon. Maeve and Jack's invitations to visit in Little Creek had to wait for another day, since Abby always seemed to get carsick after as little as an hour on the road.

Fort Meade, where Tyler worked, was completely different from the Naval Academy. Sprawling and filled with construction, Tyler had once called it an Army base that had forgotten it was Army, and she could see why. The mammoth base housed everything from the Defense Information Systems Agency to the Asymmetric Warfare Group, and even the NSA. Just making it to the parade field where the festivities were, Bess was surprised Tyler hadn't gotten lost.

Arriving an hour early to eat their picnic dinner, there was already a crowd. Tyler spotted a few people he knew sitting toward the front, and they managed to squeeze a little extra room beside them. He spread out the picnic blanket on the grass, and introduced Bess to his friends just as Abby got lassoed into a game of tag with two children.

Seeing the families with dads around them, Bess wondered if it would be good for Abby to be in this atmosphere. She had just reached that age when she started noticing that other children had dads—not just a bunch of honorary uncles like she had. How long before she started asking questions?

Even in the midst of conversation, Tyler's eyes never left Abby. Bess loved that about him. She could actually relax a little, knowing that someone else was keeping an eye out, making sure her little girl didn't wander off.

"So do you two live on base?" one of the wives asked Bess. Clarissa, Bess repeated her name silently in her head, trying to keep everyone's name straight.

"No. We're down in Annapolis."

Clarissa laughed. "Seriously? He's probably the only Army guy in that Navy town. He must really love you to let you live there, especially around game day."

The game day Clarissa referred to, Bess already knew, was Army versus Navy, one of the longest and most firmly entrenched college football rivalries out there.

"Oh no," Bess quickly corrected. "We're housemates. Just friends."

Ethan, Clarissa's husband who was holding one of Bess's fried drumsticks, piped in, "Well, in that case, can I trade in Clarissa for you? She doesn't fry chicken like this." The comment was met with a swift, but good-natured thump on the arm from his wife.

Bess grinned. "Any more comments like that, and I'm cutting off your chicken supply."

"Any more comments like that and I'll be cutting off something much more important to him than chicken," Clarissa added, firing a deadly glare at her husband.

"So, ready to be a Captain, yet?" Ethan asked Tyler.

Tyler smiled. "No, but I'm ready for the pay raise that comes with it."

Retrieving the container of chicken, Bess eyed Tyler. "You're getting promoted?"

Tyler nodded, nonchalant, as always.

She handed Tyler another drumstick. "Why didn't you tell me?"

"No big deal. I've known for months. It's just the natural course of things in the Army."

Ethan laughed. "Yeah, except he's getting promoted before me. I'll have to salute this guy for about six months till I get my own Captain's bars pinned on me. That's a damn nuisance."

Clarissa shot her husband a look. "Watch the language. There are kids around."

"Sorry," he answered her, giving his best shamed-face. "You gotta convince this guy to throw a party or something. He's being way too low-key about it. When I get promoted, I'm renting out the ballroom at the Four Seasons."

Clarissa raised an eyebrow at her husband. "And cashing out our TSP to do it, I imagine. Over my dead body. Back-yard barbeque is all you'll get, *Lieutenant.*"

Bess called Abby back over to them as the emcee announced the beginning of the program and they settled into their seats on the blanket. "Why don't we throw a party at the house, Tyler?"

"No. It's too much trouble. It's not like I'm making General, Bess. I was bound to make Captain one day. I'm not even having my mom or sister come down for it. Too long of a drive for them. I don't like making a big deal out of stuff like this."

"Yeah, but you worked hard for it. You should celebrate."

"I worked hard so I could get into Ranger Battalion. Not to get a couple bars pinned to my uniform."

"But—" Her argument was cut off by the National Anthem. Trying to get Abby to stand up for the entire length of the song proved impossible, and Bess finally lifted her little girl into her arms while she stood.

As the soprano sang, joined in by a few others in the audience, Bess glanced around. The words seemed to have more meaning to this audience than others she had seen. Tyler stood at perfect attention, and Bess felt a sense of pride at just being with him.

Promotion coming up? Didn't surprise her in the least. But if he thought she'd let him get away without having a celebration at the house afterward, then he had another thing coming to him.

After a rousing round of applause, the first part of the performance began, filled with plenty of patriotic tunes and a surprising number of classic rock songs that had Abby and the other children migrating to the front of the crowd to dance. Then a military pageant began, using Soldiers in period dress to act out scenes of war from the Revolution all the way through to the present. Muskets and cannons fired, making Abby jump and clap with glee at every earth-shaking explosion.

Just as the sun touched the horizon, the Army Drill Team marched toward them for their part of the performance. Bess's jaw dropped at their precision as they twirled and tossed M14s, real bayonets affixed. Hands down, they were

Bess's favorite part of the Twilight Tattoo, and from the wide-eyed expression on Abby's face, it was an opinion she shared with her daughter.

"How do they do that?" the little girl whispered loudly as they completed their performance.

"Years of practice," Tyler answered.

"They're like the Rockettes," Abby said in awe.

Tyler glanced at Bess. "Who are the Rockettes?"

"The chorus line tap dancers at Radio City Music Hall in New York," Bess answered. "Maeve bought her their Christmas show DVD last year."

Tyler grimaced. "Do me a favor and don't let those guys hear that, okay?"

"Promise," Bess replied with a grin. Except for the precision of their choreography, there really was no comparing the two. And she had no plans to tell a bunch of fit Soldiers holding M14s that they had just been compared to tap dancers.

When the program was complete, Bess stood to gather their things, for the first time noticing just how many people had joined the audience.

"It's so crowded," she commented. "We were lucky to be up front like this."

"Yeah, they don't travel for shows very often. Most of the time you have to go to Fort Myer in Virginia to see the Twilight Tattoo."

"Thanks so much for taking us, Tyler."

"Thank you!" Abby echoed, giving his leg a big hug.

Bess wished she could express her gratitude in the same way.

He lifted Abby into his arms. "Anytime, Peanut."

With her head now level to his, Abby gave him a kiss on the cheek, and Bess's heart felt a tug. Her little girl was growing so attached to Tyler. How would Abby handle it when he left at the end of his year here?

How would *Bess* handle it?

———

All the fresh air must have exhausted Bess. Tyler glanced over at her, her head resting against the window, eyes half shut as they filtered through the traffic to get out of Fort Meade.

"Thanks so much, Tyler," she whispered, eyes drooping.

Tyler smiled. "You already said that at least ten times, Bess. I just wish you would have let me pick up some ribs or something for the picnic. You wore yourself out cooking." As usual, Tyler added in his head. Hadn't she known that taking her to the Twilight Tattoo was supposed to be a partial payback for all the good meals?

Now, at the end of the night, he found he still owed her.

It was unexpected, he thought as he glanced at her restful face, her eyes closed. He hadn't imagined he'd have such a great time with them tonight.

If they weren't living together, he might even be tempted to ask Bess out on a date. She was fun to be around. She made him laugh. Feel comfortable.

But she was also his housemate. And the mother of the little girl he absolutely adored. He wasn't going to mess up this sweet deal to take a stab at something that would likely fail. It's not like he had banked a lot of success when it came to relationships.

Besides that, Bess didn't seem remotely interested in dating anyone right now. Being a single mom might do that to a woman, and he suspected that her relationship with Abby's father wasn't the best or he'd have at least heard the name of the guy by now.

Both Bess and Abby were out like a light by the time Tyler rolled onto the driveway. "Hey Bess. Wake up. We're home."

"Mmm. So tired."

"Yeah. You were up late last night frying chicken for the picnic," Tyler commented. "I'll put Abby to bed. You just get inside and go back to sleep. Can she skip brushing teeth tonight?"

"Mmhm," Bess said, quietly opening her car door. "Thanks, Tyler."

If she said thank you one more time to him, he'd scream. It drove him nuts.

After unsnapping the restraints in the car seat, Tyler lifted Abby into his arms. Such a warm feeling, having a little one sleeping soundly in his grasp. How could she have wrapped him so thoroughly around her finger?

Climbing the stairs, he felt Abby stirring slightly. Damn. Hope she wouldn't get fussy if she woke up.

He lowered her into her bed just as her eyes opened.

"I'm home," she noticed.

"Yep, safe and sound in your bed."

"That was fun."

"Yeah, it was."

"I like cannons. They're loud."

"They are. Now shhh. Back to sleep." He leaned over and placed a gentle kiss on Abby's forehead, deciding to let her sleep in her clothes. If she awakened too much, he suspected she'd be up all night.

"Kenny and Julie are nice."

"The kids you were playing with? Yeah, they seemed it."

"They have nice dads." She yawned. "Are you my dad?"

The question, so direct and innocent, punched him in the gut. "I'm not lucky enough to be your dad."

"Who is?"

"Ah, Abby, maybe that's more a question for your mom than for me." He sat on the bed. "But I can tell you that I never knew my own dad either."

"Really?"

"Yeah, maybe that's why we get along so well."

Abby fired him one of her chubby-cheeked grins. "We're alike. You and me."

"You and me, kiddo." He gave her a gentle high-five. "And I promise you'll always be able to count on me just like Kenny and Julie count on their dad, okay? And you've got your Uncle Mick."

"And Uncle Jack and Uncle Joe after Aunt Vi marries him next month."

"Exactly. With a bunch of guys like that looking out for you, and an amazing mom like you have, you're a really lucky girl."

"I am lucky," she murmured, her eyes fluttering shut again.

I know the feeling.

CHAPTER 7

He was a lucky son of a bitch. Tyler pounded his feet against the treadmill on a steep incline, the sweat pouring from his body. The view of the street from the room wasn't as great as looking at the Bay, but it was a damn sight nicer than the view of a concrete wall at the gym on base.

The leaves on the trees were still full and green—not many weeks left of that, he imagined—and they nearly blocked the entire quiet street from his sight. One lazy, overfed rabbit nibbled on an apple that had fallen from the tree along the driveway. He'd have to pick those apples with Abby one day. One of his favorite childhood memories was picking apples in an orchard near their small house in New York.

Bess had taken Abby to Edith's after breakfast and then would head to her catering job for the rest of the day. So the house was his for the afternoon. After his run, he'd do some paddleboarding before he showered up for his date tonight. Janette again, third date since last week, and if he was reading her right, he'd be checking out her place before the night was over.

God, it had been a while since he'd gotten laid. Nothing like the chaos of a PCS, a new post, and a three-year-old for a housemate to cramp a guy's sex life.

A red Lotus Elise pulled into the driveway. Sweet ride, Tyler thought, admiring the sleek lines of the car, and expecting it to back right out again, needing to turn around. He couldn't imagine anyone who drove a Lotus had any business at this house.

Tyler's antenna went up immediately when the car stopped. The driver stepped out of the car tentatively, looking off to both sides of the street before he approached the house. Being a Ranger, Tyler was always watching people's body language, and something about the movements of this guy definitely put him on alert.

Who the hell was this guy? And why did Tyler's gut tell him he was up to no good?

Tyler grabbed a towel and mopped off his face and bare chest, draping the towel on the back of his neck just before he heard the doorbell ring.

He opened the door. "Can I help you?"

The man took a step back, glancing briefly at Tyler's ripped chest.

Good. You better be intimidated, Tyler thought.

"Is Bess here?"

What would a guy with shifty eyes driving a Lotus want with Bess? Immediately, Tyler's protective instincts bared their fanged teeth. Hold on, Ranger, he ordered himself. Maybe this was a guy Bess had dated or something. It wasn't his place to destroy a potential relationship with one threatening glare.

"Nope," Tyler responded, his voice clipped. He certainly wasn't going to offer up any information, especially when every cell in his body was warning him the guy was trouble. "Can I help you?"

73

"Uh, no." The guy started backing away.

No way was Tyler letting him escape without finding out more. "And you are?"

"Dan. Dan Wils. Just tell her I stopped by."

Nope, he didn't like this guy at all, and he hoped to God Bess wasn't thinking he was her knight-in-shining-Lotus because there was no way Tyler would keep his opinions to himself on this matter. "Okay, Dan-Dan Wils. I'll tell her you stopped by."

Dan narrowed his eyes, a futile attempt at intimidation. Don't even try, Tyler thought, leaning against the frame of the door and folding his arms.

"Thanks," the guy responded, his tone laden with sarcasm.

Tyler loomed in the doorway till the Lotus pulled away and disappeared down the street.

Glancing at the clock on her dashboard, Bess pulled into the sprawling driveway of Edith's waterfront house. She was more than an hour late, she noted, grateful to know that Edith wouldn't mind. Bess's job with the caterer was notoriously unreliable when it came to the hours. Today's early afternoon bar mitzvah had run a lot longer than predicted, but Bess had walked away with at least three new ideas for dishes she wanted to try out on Tyler and Abby this week.

After ringing the doorbell, she was greeted by Edith's warm hug. Edith had a way of making Bess and her daughter feel so much a part of the family. Calling Edith "Grandma Edie," Abby probably hadn't even considered the possibility that the older woman wasn't her real grandmother.

"How was the bar mitzvah, dear?" Edith asked, guiding her toward the living room where Abby was settled on the floor in a pile of toys.

"Long. My feet are killing me." She was lucky to not have to wear heels, she imagined. But even the cheap black flats she had bought to go with the black pants and white shirt she was required to wear gave her blisters every time she wore them.

"Poor thing. Why don't you sit a while? Abby's happily playing with a new toy I got her."

Abby glanced up. "I want to stay, Mama."

"Five minutes," Bess conceded to her little girl, really just wanting to get home and soak her feet in the tub.

"I'm glad to have you here for a moment. We barely get a chance to talk these days."

Shame crept into Bess's heart. She did have the habit of just dropping Abby off and picking her up without really spending time with Edith. "You're right. I'm sorry."

"Oh, no. Don't be sorry at all. I just had some things I wanted to show you." Edith picked up a huge shopping bag that rested alongside the sofa. "I was shopping with Tracey yesterday."

"Tracey?"

"Yes. She's one of the mids I'm sponsoring this year. She's about your size and she picked out some adorable outfits at this new store at the mall. I've never heard of the place before, so that must mean it's very trendy." She laughed. "Anyway, I picked up a few things for you."

"Me? Oh, Edith, that's really nice. But I can't afford to buy new clothes right now. I've got a quarterly payment due for Abby's preschool coming up this month."

"Oh, no, dear. They're my gift to you," she clarified as she plopped the heavy bag onto Bess's lap.

Bess's eyes widened. "That's so sweet. But you shouldn't be buying me gifts. You already do so much for me."

"I do it because I want to. And I'm too old to argue with. Take a look."

Bess bit her lip as she pulled out the first item. She could only imagine the kind of clothes a woman old enough to be her grandmother would pick out for her. So she was a little stunned to see a couple of skin-tight workout shirts and two pairs of yoga pants, the kind that hug every curve.

"I thought those might be nice to hang around the house in. Sort of a step up from your old sweats, don't you think?"

Bess couldn't argue with her. They were really nice, and the material would feel so light and comfortable against her skin, even though she worried they might make her look like an elephant. Feeling the weight of more items inside the bag, she reached in again and pulled out a body-hugging casual dress with a built-in bra and spaghetti straps. *Holy crap. This thing is downright sexy.*

"Don't you love it?" Edith exclaimed in her usual bubbly tone. "It will really show off your figure."

What figure? Was Edith referring to Bess's rippling waistline or her butt that had succumbed to the Earth's gravitational pull?

"It's beautiful, Edith. I don't know that they'll fit, though."

"Oh, I think they will. You've been losing so much weight with all that working out you've been doing."

"You think I'm losing weight?"

Edith cocked her head. "Yes, dear. You have. You might not have realized it since everything you own has an elastic waistband." The slight grin on Edith's face took a hint of the sting away from the comment. "Now I realize that it might be a new low for you to get fashion advice from a 70-something matron like me, but you really do need to start showing off all your hard work on that treadmill."

Bess laughed. "Okay, okay. I'll try them on when I get home. I promise. And thanks, Edith. It's really so generous of you." She gave her a kiss on the cheek.

"Oh, it's nothing. I'd buy more for you if I thought you'd

accept it," Edith said, taking Abby by the hand. "Come along now, Abby. Let's get your mommy home so she can soak those sore feet in a hot bath, okay? I'm buying you better shoes next, Bess. Whether you like it or not."

"Are your feet hurt, Mama?" the little girl asked Bess as Edith walked her out the door and toward the car.

"Just a little. I'll be okay. Give Grandma Edie a hug now."

Abby embraced Edith with a full body hug. "Love you."

"Love you, too, sweetheart," Edith answered, helping Abby into her car seat and snapping it tight.

Bess gave a wave to Edith as she pulled out of the driveway, thinking about the bag of clothes she had just tossed into the back seat. She wasn't even sure if she had the nerve to try them on, as tight fitting as they were. But she would. She had promised.

The sun was low in the sky as she drove over the Naval Academy Bridge, and a group of midshipmen caught her eye as they took their evening run.

She remembered the first time she had run on Tyler's treadmill, only lasting a whopping ninety seconds. She hadn't improved much since then—barely able to top off five minutes before her knees started killing her. But her walking had definitely improved. She could keep up a 4.4 mile per hour pace for fifteen minutes before having to slow it down to an easier to maintain four miles an hour.

Could she really have lost a little weight? She'd never admit it, but Edith had been right. Bess tended to opt for clothes that were stretchy. The kind of items a girl could gain ten pounds in without even feeling it.

She wasn't eating nearly like she used to, either. She had always been such a stress eater, but now that she was working out almost daily, she found herself a lot more relaxed.

With her shopping bag in hand, she opened the door,

watching Abby shoot up the stairs like a bullet. "Brush your teeth and get ready for your bath now, okay?" Bess commanded.

Silence ensued, as it usually did when Bess was handing out a task to her three-year-old.

"Did you hear me, Abby? Abby?"

"What?" Abby called downstairs.

"I said to brush your teeth and get ready for your bath. I'll be up in a few minutes. Okay?"

"Okay."

Bess sighed, tossing the bag on the sofa along with herself. It would be a half hour before Abby got those two things done, and she knew it. She kicked off her shoes. Might as well enjoy the time off.

"Hey," Tyler said as he came down the stairs, looking decadent. The cobalt color of the polo shirt seemed to make his blue eyes pop, and its short sleeves stopped just high enough to showcase his marvelous biceps. He was wearing khaki pants tonight rather than jeans, a step up in this casual town of Annapolis. He must have a date, Bess thought, feeling a tinge of jealousy.

"Hey, yourself. You look great. What are you dressed up for?"

"Taking Janette out to dinner and to hear some music in Baltimore. I'll be pretty late. Thought I should tell you so you didn't worry."

"Oh, I wouldn't worry. Someone living in this house has to get some action," Bess laughed, hoping her sense of humor would lighten up her mood.

"You gotta get out and meet some guys, Bess. You're around the house too much."

"I'm a mom, Tyler. That's what happens."

"Oh, hey, speaking of... some guy stopped by to see you."

Bess shrugged. "Probably the guy who raked the leaves last year looking for work."

Tyler laughed. "Not driving a Lotus. No, don't think he was raking leaves for a living. Dan something." He paused briefly. "Dan Wils."

Tasting the burn of bile in her mouth, her body seized up in panic.

"Oh, God." She was hot suddenly, dizzy, desperately needing to empty her stomach. She rose, staggered a moment as Tyler reached for her to help, and darted across the room to the bathroom. Her full body quaked and she hugged the toilet. Nothing came, just a sizzling in her esophagus. Her heart was racing.

With Tyler standing behind her, she felt too sick to even be humiliated, half-collapsed on the bathroom.

"Bess, what's wrong?"

A whirring sound echoed deep inside her ears as pressure built in her skull, the sound so deafening she could barely hear him.

"Oh, God." She pulled herself back from the toilet, but was too weak to stand. Her skin felt clammy and her sight was blurred. Deep breaths, she told herself. *Abby's upstairs. I have to keep it together.*

A red Lotus, she suddenly thought, remembering. The same damn car she had seen twice now and blamed her own frayed nerves and ample imagination.

Oh, God. Had he seen Abby? Even the thought of him being so close to her daughter made her sick. Finally, she dared to look at Tyler. Had he really said it? The one name that could send her into a fit of terror?

Tyler reached for a washcloth and wetted it in the sink. He wrung it out, and pressed it against Bess's forehead as he sat next to her on the ground.

"So Dan Wils is not a nice guy," he concluded.

Bess knew an answer was unnecessary. Lucky for that, because she still couldn't form words.

"Are you with me, Bess? Do you need to lie down?"

Dan. He knew where she was. But how? Had he contacted her parents? Had they said something? She felt a chill of betrayal from the possibility. She had never told her parents how Dan had beaten her, and hadn't dared to admit to them that Abby was his child. But she had specifically told them that she never wanted to see him again.

"How did he find me?" she heard herself say out loud.

Tyler frowned. "In the age of the internet, anyone can find anybody if they try hard enough." He paused, probably waiting for her to offer something more. But when she said nothing, he asked, "Old boyfriend?"

In an instant, sitting on the bathroom floor, she was transported to another moment in time. When Dan had come home drunk from a night out with his friends, and he had accused Bess of going out someplace without him. She hadn't left the apartment at all that night, wouldn't have dared to. She had known by then that jealousy was one of his worst triggers. She denied it, and went to the bathroom to get ready for bed. He had followed her in and pushed her into the wall, calling her a string of obscenities, punching her and then knocking her down to the floor, kicking her in the stomach before he finally walked away.

Sitting on the floor now, her hands shook convulsively at the memory.

"Abusive old boyfriend," she heard Tyler clarify for himself. "Fucking bastard," he added, his fists clenching.

A biting chill swept over Bess as she finally found her voice. "I have to get out of here."

"What do you mean?"

"I have to get out of Annapolis."

"You can't leave the life you have here just because some

old boyfriend has come back to cause trouble. You'll be running your whole life, if you do that."

"You don't understand." She could barely see Tyler behind the film of tears forming in her eyes.

"I *do* understand. And I know that *I'm* living in this house and he won't lay a hand on you without having it ripped off first by me."

"You don't understand," Bess repeated, keeping her voice quiet. Please stay upstairs, she silently willed her daughter. *Please give Mama a little time to figure out what to do.*

Tyler stood and extended a hand to pull her up. "Okay, so enlighten me." He walked her out to the back porch, probably thinking the same thing she was—that Abigail didn't need to hear what was going on.

Sitting in the cushioned chair, she leaned forward, still pressing the cool washcloth to her face to dull the pain behind her eyes. After a few deep breaths, she set it aside and looked out to the Bay to soothe her soul. "Dan is Abby's father."

Tyler shut his eyes. "Shit. Does he know?"

"No. I left him the day I found out I was pregnant. I had already distanced myself from my friends and family in Pennsylvania. Dan didn't like or trust any of them. He liked keeping me to himself, you know?"

"Trait of an abusive man."

"Guess so. So anyway, it was the summer before my senior year. We had been living together for a few months. I don't know why I stayed with him," she felt compelled to add. How could anyone understand why someone would stay with a man like Dan? Even going home to her rotten parents for the summer would have been a better option than shacking up with that bastard. "It's so embarrassing."

"You shouldn't be embarrassed. You should just be proud

that you finally left. Guys like that are masters at manipulation, Bess."

Finally looking at him, she nodded. "That's it. That's it exactly. I kept feeling like the abuse was my fault. That if I could just be a better girlfriend, it would all work out." Bess thought of her parents and saw the pattern. If she could just be a better daughter. If she could just be a better girlfriend. She had stepped from the frying pan into the fire.

"But it didn't."

"No. Definitely not. The day I did the pregnancy test, suddenly nothing else mattered except protecting my child from him. I realized that I couldn't fix Dan. So that day when he went to work, I packed my bags and left."

"He had no idea where you went?"

Bess shook her head. "I left a note saying I was leaving town for a few months. I told him he'd be better off without me—you know—so I wouldn't enrage him too much."

"What did you tell your parents?"

Bess actually laughed a little—probably not the reaction Tyler was expecting. "I told them I was going to Europe with some friends from college for the rest of the summer." Shaking her head, she rolled her eyes. "They never asked any questions, like where I was staying or how I'd get the money to survive. And when the summer ended, I didn't hear a word from them either. They've never given a damn."

"How did you end up here?"

Bess squeezed the knotted muscles in her neck. "I drove down to Annapolis—it was literally one tank of gas, I remember—and I stopped at a station to fill up the car. I didn't know where I was going. I had pulled out all the money I could from bank machines in Pennsylvania before I left, just in case Dan figured out a way to get information out of the bank, you know?"

"Smart thinking."

"I got a room at that motel off I-97 and stayed there for a couple weeks while I answered some ads for people needing housecleaning. That's how I heard about Maeve's house. I cleaned a couple of her neighbors' homes and they vouched for me. So I was living with Maeve within the month."

Tyler leaned forward. "And you haven't heard from him? Up till today, that is."

"No. I was kind of off the grid for a while there, and I've tried to keep it that way as much as possible. Even now, with Maeve gone, I still keep all the electric bills in her name. But it's harder when you have a kid, you know. When she started day care, there were a lot of forms to fill out. Maybe something got online that way."

"We can find out easily enough. I'll look you up online tonight and see what pops up."

Bess sighed. "Or it might have been my parents. That's what really scares me. Because about a year after Abby was born, I decided to contact them. I don't know why. They sure hadn't wanted to be in touch with me. But there was part of me that just felt like they might want to know they had a grandchild."

"You'd think." Sarcasm laced his tone. "I take it they didn't turn into the grandparents of your dreams?"

"No. They thought I was going to ask them for money. Told me that I had made my own bed, and now I had to lie in it."

"Wow, tough love at its worst."

Bess heard a call from upstairs. "Mama, I'm naked!"

Bess almost grinned from the sound of her little girl's voice. Almost, but not quite, as a fresh crop of tears filled her eyes.

"I'll be right up for bath time, honey." Bess's voice cracked with emotion as she tried to stand, wavering a little, still lightheaded.

"I'm walking you up there. Can't she skip bath tonight?"

Forcing a small smile, Bess sighed. "She'll love you for life if she hears you suggest that."

Tyler took her face in his hands and Bess felt an unexpected surge of warmth that tamed the icy clutches of fear that had been clenching her heart. "You're not going anywhere," he said. "Understand? Let's get Abby to bed, and we'll talk more after."

"You have a date," she reminded him.

"*Had* a date. I'll cancel. This is more important."

"You don't have to," Bess protested.

Tyler cocked his head to the side. "There's no way I'm leaving you and Abby alone tonight. If Janette doesn't understand, then she's probably not the right girl for me."

Bess stared at him a moment, almost lost in eyes that seemed to offer her such hope, before turning to go back inside.

Whoever *was* the right girl for him was a damn lucky woman.

CHAPTER 8

Mick leaned back in his chair in the windowless office at the Pentagon, his eyes deadly at the news. "Did you figure out how he might have found her?"

Tyler gave a curt nod. "Cell phone. Bess uses a burner phone, and the number's unlisted. But she puts it on her credit card, so one of those people-finder services has her listed."

"Still, it could have been her parents."

"That's just it. We don't know. And most importantly, we don't know if he knows about Abby."

Mick narrowed his eyes. "Where are they now?"

"I told Bess to take the day off work and keep Abby out of preschool today. They went to Edith's house."

"Good idea."

"I did a little research online and it looks like he just started a job up in Gaithersburg. So moving to the area might have been the push for him to show up on Bess's front stoop now as opposed to a couple years ago. I found his address."

"Apartment or house?"

"Apartment. Drove by it this morning."

Mick folded his hands in front of him. "What kind of security?"

"Nil. No doorman or intercom. I can waltz right up to his door."

"Handy."

Tyler nodded. "He's got a police record. Looked it up last night. Seems Bess wasn't the only girl he knocked around."

"Good," Mick said, and clarified when he saw Tyler's eyes widen in response. "Good that he has a record. Bess never went to the cops. And if he does try to get some kind of custody of Abby, we can use that against him."

"Exactly. But right now, I just want to find out more. Like does he know about Abby? And if he does, does he know that he's her father?" Tyler pressed his lips together thoughtfully for a moment. "If he doesn't know about Abby, I might be able to just scare him away. From the look on his face, he had no idea I was living with Bess. He looked like he was going to shit his pants when I opened the door."

"That'd be my guess, too. What's the build on this guy?"

"Nothing I can't handle."

Mick raised his eyebrows. "Assholes like that have weapons. Don't get too cocky."

"I'm a Ranger. I'd take him down before he could grab anything and you know it."

"Did you talk to Bess about going to the police?"

"Yeah. She doesn't want to yet. And I kind of agree. He hasn't done anything yet."

"He only beat up his girlfriend multiple times," Mick responded with sarcasm.

"Four years ago and in a different state. If we get the police involved, he'll probably find out about Abby."

"That's what it all comes down to. If he doesn't know about Abby, we should keep it that way." Mick leaned back in his chair, eyes still locked on Tyler. "So you're suggesting a little reconnaissance mission?"

"Yep. Needed your input though. I don't want to go off half-cocked. You've got a few missions under your belt," Tyler said, glancing at the ample medals pinned to Mick's chest. "To say the least."

"I think you're right to confront him. Catch him off guard. Get the info we need. Scare the hell out of him. And leave. I'm coming with you."

"No, Sir."

Mick angled a look at Tyler that would make any other man turn to ice.

"Respectfully, Sir. I need to do this alone. If I show up with you, he probably won't even open the door. Plus, he's never seen you. We can hold that card to our chest and maybe use it another day."

"You're good at this." Mick glanced away thoughtfully, his eyes resting momentarily on the picture of Lacey he had on his desk. "Okay, I'll just drive you. If I don't see you come out of his apartment in, say, four minutes, I bust the door in."

Tyler cracked a smile. "That'd fix the guy."

Mick grinned back. "Yeah, but also would attract too much attention. So just get out of there in four minutes, okay? Bess would have my hide if you got hurt. She says you're a great housemate and really good to Abby." Mick took a sip from the coffee mug that had been sitting on his desk, grimacing slightly from the taste. "Thanks for that, by the way."

Tyler shrugged in response. "She's good to me. I've never eaten better in my life. And Abby? Hell, that little girl's a peach." He paused a moment, then added. "Not planning on letting anyone hurt them. Not on my watch."

Mick set down the mug. "So have you thought about how

you'll get the information out of him without him slamming the door in your face?"

"I've got a plan."

"I'm all ears."

Logic told Tyler that he should feel an adrenaline rush from the prospect of confrontation. Yet after facing armed terrorists and insurgents, Dan Wils hardly registered as a blip on his radar screen.

"You're sure this is where he lives?" Mick asked, doing a full circle around the perimeter of the apartment complex, eyes searching, probably for security cameras.

Tyler spotted Dan's Lotus parked outside one of the two-story buildings. "Yep. That's his car." He jotted down the license plate number, in case it might come in handy down the road.

"The guy drives a Lotus and lives in a place like this?" Mick shook his head, probably picturing the same thing Tyler was—massive monthly payments for a car that was begging to get vandalized in exposed parking.

Dan Wils was as stupid as he looked. Which, Tyler thought, could only work to their advantage.

"Okay," Mick said, pulling into a space just barely within sight of the apartment door Tyler had been eyeing. "Let me see your watch." He synchronized his with Tyler's and set the alarm on his own for four minutes. "I'm pressing the start button the second you walk in that door. So don't get chatty with the son of a bitch. Find out what we need to know and get out. And no beating the shit out of him, Tyler. We don't need the police showing up on your doorstep. Got it?"

"Okay, Dad," Tyler grumbled, hoping to God that the guy took a swing at him so that he'd have the excuse to defend himself. Just one punch is all it would take to hopefully scare this guy out of Bess's life.

Tyler stepped out of the car and walked up to the door, glancing to both sides of him before he knocked. Not a soul around or a security camera in sight. So that he couldn't be visible through the peephole, he stepped to the side of the door. As expected, Dan opened it.

Tyler slipped his foot against the frame of the door. There was no slamming it shut on a steel-toed Army boot.

Dan's eyes were wary at the sight of Tyler in uniform. "What the fuck are you doing here?"

Tyler smiled. "You were nice enough to pay me a visit at my place. Thought I'd return the favor."

"What do you want?"

"A few minutes of your time. I think we have something in common."

"I don't have shit in common with you."

Tyler cocked his head. "Really? Then you were looking for a different Bess when you showed up on my doorstep?"

"Fuck you." He tried to shut the door, and it stopped on Tyler's boot.

"That's fine, chickenshit. We can talk right here," Tyler said, raising his voice. "Air your dirty laundry out so that your neighbors can enjoy it."

Dan stared at him a moment, glancing briefly over Tyler's uniform, no doubt wondering if he had some kind of weapon. *You bet I have a weapon.* Two actually, Tyler thought, willing his fists to not form yet. Can't scare the guy too much if he wanted an invitation inside.

Dan opened the door. "Get in. I'll give you two minutes before I'm calling the cops."

Yeah, right.

Tyler stepped inside and looked around. Pretty much looked like a typical apartment for a single guy, with a brown sectional that was likely older than its present owner, and a papasan chair. The mismatched, second-hand furniture, though, seemed inconsistent with the state-of-the-art widescreen TV that could barely fit the wall. Between the TV and the car, Tyler was starting to suspect Dan might be leading a lifestyle he couldn't afford.

"What do you want?" Dan said, shutting the door behind Tyler.

"Simple. I want to know why you were sniffing around my house and my woman." Tyler answered possessively, playing the role of the protective boyfriend, which he figured would be the best way to keep the guy away from Bess.

"I was in town. Wanted to see how she was. We had a thing a few years back." Dan stalked backwards a few steps from Tyler, crossing his arms over his chest.

"Yeah, and I know you beat her when you were together. You have to know, I don't like people who do that, Dan-Dan."

Dan leaned casually against the back of his couch. "Is that what she told you? You're a fool, man. You can't believe a girl like Bess. She'll say anything for attention. She likes it rough, you know. Then she can cry about it later."

"So if she's such a lying bitch, why'd you look her up?"

Dan shrugged. "You'll do the same when she screws you over like she did me. I just wanted to scare her a little. But if you want her, she's all yours. Now get the fuck out of my place before I call the cops."

Tyler couldn't resist the laugh that escaped him. "You'll call the cops? I wonder whose side they'd take. Some lowlife with a police record, or a decorated Soldier?"

Dan looked uneasy, probably from the mention of his police record. "So what do you want?"

Stepping toward him, Tyler angled him a deadly gaze. "I want you to stay away from my house and my woman. You got that? If I see you sniffing around again, they'll never find your body."

"You're fucking crazy."

Tyler scoffed. "I'm a Ranger, asshole. It's a whole special brand of crazy. And we get a little pissed when guys like you hurt women. You just keep remembering how fucking crazy I am the next time you get the itch to find out what Bess is up to."

Turning toward the door, Tyler knew Dan would try to strike him when he wasn't looking. Guys like this were so predictable. When he felt him close in, Tyler ducked his head, spun around, and kicked him in the gut right before planting his fist in Dan's face.

Dan fell to the floor.

"911, buddy. Call them right away," Tyler advised Dan, knowing damn well he wouldn't. "You remember what I said, Dan-Dan. You're being watched. I called a friend with the police. They've got your plate number. They'll be looking out for you. Anything weird happens within a five mile radius of Bess and it'll be pinned on you, believe me." He stood, pinning his boot against Dan's chest much more lightly than he would have preferred. "You go on with your life, and I'll let you live. You come around Bess again, and I'll seriously fuck you up."

After walking away, Tyler shut the door behind him, pain radiating from the fist he had acquainted with Dan's face. It had been overkill. He could have sent him to the floor with lesser a blow. But damn, it had felt good to feel the guy's cheekbone crunch against his hand.

Climbing into Mick's car, the questioning happened fast. "Does he know about Abby?"

Tyler grinned. "Nope. He didn't mention her at all. And believe me, he would have."

Relief washed over Mick's face, making Tyler realize the Commander cared as much about that little girl as Tyler did.

"Call Bess right away," he said, handing him his cell.

Tyler winced a little when he took the phone in his grip, his hand already swelling slightly from the impact.

Mick narrowed his eyes on Tyler's hand. "I told you not to beat him up."

Tyler shrugged. "What could I do? He hit my fist with his face."

Pulling out of the parking lot, Mick laughed.

CHAPTER 9

Bess stood in front of the sink in her new white gi. Not her usual attire for scraping the remnants of chicken piccata off the skillet, but Abby was hungry and she hadn't had time to change after getting home from the gym.

After his run-in with Dan, Tyler had insisted Bess join his MMA gym and learn some self-defense. Just once, he said, and she'd be hooked.

She hadn't believed him, of course.

Her first class was on Monday. Basic self-defense for women. By the end of the hour, she was drenched in sweat, her throat was sore from practicing her shouting, and her legs throbbed from kicking.

What an awesome way to start the week, she had decided, feeling more powerful than she ever had.

On Tuesday, after waking up with her muscles screaming in agony, she thought a night off would be a good idea. But Abby had begged to go back again that evening because in the gym's child care facility they had a bouncer for the kids up on Tuesdays, and what child could resist that?

So Bess had decided to suffer through a kickboxing class for an hour while Abby bounced to her heart's content.

"Kickboxing is freaking awesome!!!" she had texted Lacey and Maeve from the locker room at the end of the class.

Then today, one of the gym's owners, Connor, had greeted Bess and Abby at the door with a gi. She'd need a gi, he explained, for tonight's women's grappling course.

Grappling? She had thought the idea crazy. It was one thing to punch target mitts or kick a heavy bag, but an actual person?

But when Connor told her that Tyler had bought her the gi, she had been so ridiculously touched by the gesture, she couldn't refuse.

Before Bess knew what had happened, she found herself rolling around on the mats, trying to break free and pass the guard of another student. Not just *trying* to—but actually *learning how* to. How many times would that have come in handy in her relationship with Dan?

She was hooked.

"Hey, look at you!" Tyler exclaimed as he walked in through the door and looked Bess up and down in her gi. Abby jumped up from the table and crawled up Tyler's tall form like he was a ladder.

"Do you like it?" Bess asked, biting her lip.

"Yeah. You look like you're ready for a cage fight." Giving Abby a kiss on the forehead, he set her back down in her chair.

"I'm not ready for that yet. But I did take the grappling class today." Bess handed him a plate of chicken piccata she had saved for him. "Thanks for the gi, Tyler. That was really so sweet. I want to pay you back for it, though."

"I'll never let you. I've always wanted to watch a woman cook me dinner in a gi. It's a little fantasy of mine." Eyes suddenly widening, he darted a look at Abby as though he might be assessing whether that comment had been too much for an inquisitive three-year-old to hear. When she kept eating her chicken, his shoulders dropped in relief and he shot a smile at Bess. "She's eating chicken," he noticed.

Bess nodded. "Gave up the vegetarian thing when I fried up some bacon the other day."

"Yeah, I'm with you, Abby. Hard to resist bacon." Tyler sat next to Abby. "So did you like class?"

Bess knew her grin must seem a mile wide. "It was incredible."

Tyler laughed. "Good for you. I thought you'd like that one. The kind of fighting you learn in that class is really the most like reality. Fights end up on the ground." He took a bite of the chicken piccata and his eyes dropped to half-mast in appreciation. "Oh, this is so good. I'll buy you a new gi every week for a meal like this. And how are you liking the child care there, Abby?"

"It's fun. They had a bouncer yesterday."

Tyler nodded. "I know. They have it up on Thursdays, too. I wish I could use it." He faked a frown.

Abby giggled. "You're too big. You'd pop it."

"You're right, I probably would."

Abby squirmed down from her chair. "Done, Mama."

Bess smiled at the sight of her daughter's nearly empty plate. Her appetite had definitely increased after an hour on that bouncer. "Then go upstairs and get ready for your bath."

"Okay."

No argument today. Or yesterday. Apparently, going to the gym after work agreed with Abby, too. She wore herself out and seemed actually anxious to go to bed.

"So you like the gym?" Tyler asked after Abby had disappeared up the stairs.

Bess rinsed off Abby's plate and loaded it into the dishwasher. "Like you need to ask? I'm loving it. I don't understand why I get to go for free on your membership, though." She narrowed her eyes slightly, bracing herself for whatever lie might follow.

Tyler waffled. "Um, the kind of membership I have allows for a spouse. And since I didn't have a spouse they just let me put you on there with me. Are these little brown things capers?" he asked, clearly trying to distract her.

Raising her eyebrows, she ignored the question. "Really? That's interesting, since I asked at the front desk and they said that you were actually paying extra for me."

Tyler lowered his head, swallowing a curse. "I told them to keep that quiet. Look, I'm sorry, but I just figured it was my responsibility, since I'm the one who is pretty much forcing you to go."

"You're not forcing me. It was a good idea."

"Good. I'm glad. The matter is closed, then." He shoved a fork full of chicken into his mouth.

"No, not till you let me pay you back every month for this."

"Denied," he responded, his voice muffled with a mouth full of food. "Bess, I'm saving so much money by staying here. Seriously. It's a ton less than those apartments I was looking at. Plus, you're always cooking for me. Hell, you even do my laundry half the time, though I wish to God you wouldn't 'cause I know my PTs smell like ass after a workout."

"Won't you let me at least—"

"No," he cut her off, looking ten times as stubborn as her temperamental three-year-old.

Bess stood there, feeling the need to argue the point further, but unable to form words. He was… taking care of her again. Protecting her. Helping her. It was an odd sensation, one that seemed to send her hormones racing through her veins like an Olympic bobsledding team. "Okay, then," she finally said. "Thanks, Tyler. More than I can say." She sighed, giving his arm a squeeze, yet desperately craving more contact with him than that.

"My pleasure."

She brushed down the front of her gi and gave a little twirl. "So do I look intimidating in my gi?"

Tyler raised an eyebrow. "Well, you'd look a lot more intimidating if you hadn't tied the belt wrong."

"I tied the belt wrong?"

"Yep. There's a whole art to doing it."

"No kidding?"

"Let me show you. First, uhh—never put a bow in it." He gave an adorable snort. "Makes you totally look amateur. I can't believe someone didn't correct you before you walked out of the gym."

"But it's so long. If I just tie a knot in it, it will drag on the ground."

Tyler came over to her and started untying the belt. Her heart rate spiked as the front of her gi opened to him. She had a t-shirt on underneath, like all the other women at the gym wore under their gis. Yet still, the idea of him undressing her in any way made her feel like there were fiery torches surging through her bloodstream.

"There's a couple ways to tie your belt," he explained. "The easy way is to first find the middle." He folded the belt at its center so that his right hand was holding the fold. His other hand grasped hers and joined it with his own, holding the belt.

The feel of his skin against hers made her dizzy.

"You do it yourself, Bess. Muscle memory is best for these things," he explained. He held his hand over hers as he guided her. "Now put the center right here," he said, pressing his hand and hers up against her belly button, "and wrap it around to the back." His face was so close to hers as he wrapped his arms around her, that she could smell the chicken piccata on his breath.

His arms were completely encircled around her waist and held her hands behind her, so that Bess could feel the pressure of his chest against her breasts.

She swallowed. Hard. This was more than she could handle.

"Now switch hands in the back, and pull it back to the front."

His hands were back at her belly again, after she did as she had been told, and she ached to feel the pressure of his chest against her again.

"The left side goes over them both, and then tucks underneath." He pushed slightly against her belly as he tucked the belt in, making her breath hitch. "Now see this one?" He grabbed hold of one end. "You take the one that is sort of flopping over the belt and you tie it again." He ran his hand along the belt, making sure it was smooth, and then gave the knot a tug. "See?"

Bess was breathless. And addicted. *More, please.*

She bit her lip. "You said there's another way to do it?"

"Uh, yeah. You want to learn it?"

Bess gulped, nodding. Hell, yeah, if it meant feeling his arms wrapped around her again.

How long had it been since she had felt such a sensation? Years. An entire lifetime ago, literally. Abby's lifetime. She had been too frightened to get close to anyone since Dan. Except for the brotherly hugs she got from Mick and Jack, she hadn't allowed any kind of closeness to a man. And this sensation was entirely different. So different it stunned her.

"Okay. So this is usually how the black belts do it. Take this end in your hand." Again, his hand enclosed over hers as she held the end of the belt in her grip. He pressed their hands into her hip. "And put it right here. Now I want you to wrap it all the way around your body."

His arms encircled her again and she glanced up, her mouth so close to his that there was no escaping the pull. Inhaling sharply, she touched her lips to his.

Eyes widening, as though she had no idea what she had just done, she pulled her lips from his barely an inch before the feeling of complete shame set in… until he moved his mouth back to hers and let his warm lips consume her.

Dropping the belt, his hands moved to her face, tracing gently along her jawline to her ears, then tunneling into her hair. She heard what she could only call a low growl and had no idea whether the sound came from him or her.

Breathing in deep, her chest rose against him, and her hands moved to his back, uncertain where to go. His lips gently grazed over hers as he coaxed her mouth open. Then she tasted him, felt the slickness of his tongue as he tentatively explored her, sliding it along her teeth. Dipping into him, she intermingled her own tongue with his.

It was such a sensation. For a woman who had so long been in the desert, it was like drinking a 6'1" glass of ice water. Not lasting more then ten seconds, she was ready to beg for more, when she heard two words that sent her careening back to reality.

"I'm ready!" Abby called from upstairs.

Tyler lurched back from Bess as though he had just pressed his lips to a hot stove. "Oh, crap," he said. "I'm sorry. Don't know what the hell just happened there."

Bess pressed her hand against her mouth. "No. That was totally my fault. I don't know what got into me."

"No, no. I shouldn't have…" His voice trailed as his eyes squinted slightly, as though trying to remember exactly what had just happened.

"It was my fault. I made the first move. It wasn't you at all.

I'm so sorry." Bess couldn't help it. Tears pooled in her eyes. "It's just... I don't know." She wiped her eyes. "I'll be up in a second honey," she called to Abby.

"Bess, oh God. Don't cry about it. Hell, this was the best part of my day," he joked, obviously trying to lighten the mood.

"I feel like an idiot. I don't know what's with me. I just haven't—" She shook her head, tears flowing. "It's been so long since... Oh, God. I'm so sorry. I guess I just haven't kissed a man in so long, and there you were, you know? Your face so close to mine. I just wanted to remember what it felt like, I guess."

Tyler's face softened, and he moved toward her again, securing a lock of her hair behind her ear. "You haven't dated at all since Dan?"

"It's embarrassing, isn't it? Four years." She kept her voice hushed. "I kept using Abby as an excuse. But really, I was just scared. I still am, but now it's different. Now I'm scared I've forgotten, you know, how to even be with a man. How to even kiss a man. And there you were, Tyler. Your lips just inches away, and I just..." Her voice trailed, mortified. "So stupid. You must think I'm a basket case, Tyler. I'm so sorry about this."

"Mama!"

"I'm not. I got to kiss a pretty lady out of the deal." Tyler grinned as Bess stepped toward the stairs. "But if you start demanding more than a kiss from me, I might just ask you to get a sitter first."

Casually, he gave her a wink before she climbed the stairs.

If she didn't have her child to bathe, she'd most definitely crawl into a dark hole until shame wore off.

Think about baseball. Isn't that what they always said would kill a raging hard-on? But the only home run he could imagine right now was with his hot housemate.

Hearing the water running upstairs, he was grateful for at least the next fifteen or twenty minutes to himself while Abby got her bath. Grabbing a beer from the fridge, he headed out to the back porch. It was a pretty cool night for September in Annapolis, he noticed. Or maybe that was just because any air would feel cold right now against his skin, after being heated thoroughly by the feel of Bess's lips on his.

He wanted her. That's what was killing him. She was cute, with those big blue eyes and fiery hair. Easy to talk to. She made him smile. There was a fierce determination in her that he could relate to. And she was a hell of a mother to Abby.

Simply put, the girl had every characteristic a woman needed to unleash the alpha wolf in him, ready to protect her with all he was.

Top that off with the fact that she could cook, and what guy wouldn't think she was the jackpot of all women?

He tossed back a healthy gulp of Sam Adams, hoping the chill of it would head straight south.

She shouldn't feel bad at all for making the first move. With his arms wrapped around her as he helped her with her belt, it took all the control he'd had not to initiate the kiss himself. And he sure as hell didn't have the excuse she did. He wasn't recovering from an abusive ex and a four-year time-out from the opposite sex.

Four years? That was just plain unnatural.

Yet at the same time, he felt somehow aroused by it. How fucked up was that? All he kept thinking about was how much he'd like to show her just how incredible sex could be. Give him one night with her and he'd make her never want to go without again.

Down, boy.

He shook his head out to the horizon.

"Not possible," he heard himself say out loud.

And a hushed voice seemed to gently wash over the waves and creep into his head.

And why not?

CHAPTER 10

"Hey, Tyler."

Headed across the mats toward the door, a voice behind Tyler stopped him.

Connor, one of the instructors at the MMA gym, loped toward him. He was a tall guy, like Tyler, with the build of a fighter.

"Yeah, Connor. What's up?"

"Bess was in class a lot last week."

"Yep. She's liking it."

Connor grinned. "She's a helluva fireplug. A lot of energy packed into a tiny frame. And her kicks are incredible. I subbed for Lou in kickboxing and she nearly sent me to the ground."

"Yeah, I know." And what of it? Tyler couldn't help wonder. It was probably just Connor's appreciation as an instructor that he was showing. Tyler had taught Troops some of the MMA skills that translated well in the field. He knew how satisfying it was to have a student excel under his wing.

"Are you and she dating or something?" Connor asked. "I

know her membership is listed under your credit card number so I was kind of wondering."

"No," Tyler said quickly. "We're just friends. Housemates. You know," he responded carelessly.

"Oh, good."

Tyler gave a nod, and was about to push open the door when he stopped and turned around again. "Why good?"

"I was gonna ask her out sometime."

Tyler stood there, slightly slack-jawed, and not from the right hook he took in the ring just before he had hit the showers that night.

"She's got a kid, you know," Tyler found himself saying. Yeah, that was it. Tyler wasn't jealous. He was just worried about Bess and Abby. He'd known Connor only a couple months or so, and he seemed like a pretty good guy. Not the kind to sleep around and then brag about his conquests in the locker room. Or talk about women like they were something meant to be used and thrown away. Connor might actually be good for Bess—another tough guy at the ready to beat the shit out of Dan if he ever bared his ugly face in this town again.

But Bess had a little girl who was depending on her. Bess didn't need to be dicked around.

"I know. Abby. I see her in the child care room when Bess comes in for class. Great kid." Connor cocked his head. "So you don't mind if I ask her out, right?"

Tyler stood there a moment, trying to get the answer to form on his lips. Connor would be good for Bess. Good for Abby.

But I'd be better.

Shit. How the hell had he let this happen? Bess was his housemate. And even more importantly, his friend. If he dared to go down this road, and it didn't work out, he'd be stuck living the remainder of his one-year lease with someone who might very well detest him after the tailspin of a break-up. And he'd lose the friend he'd gotten pretty used to having.

Besides that, if things went sour between them, how would he stay in Abby's life?

"Tyler?"

Tyler snapped out of the internal debate that was echoing in his brain. "Yeah?"

"Is there something going on between you two? You're a helluva fighter. I don't want to piss you off."

Tyler laughed at that. Connor had trained in Muay Thai kickboxing in Thailand, competed professionally there, and was a BJJ brown belt. Tyler might be a contender in the ring with him on a good day, but Connor didn't exactly have to worry about pissing off Tyler—or anyone else in this gym.

But it spoke well of Connor that he'd even say such a thing. A lot of guys would just move in on any woman without thinking twice about whether or not a friend was interested in her. He was a good guy.

Giving an internal nod, Tyler finally said, "No. No, really. Go for it. She's a great person. You can't do better than Bess, believe me." He could feel his face frowning as he said it, not exactly reflecting the sentiment he was trying to convey.

Furrowing his sweaty brow, Connor took a step back. "Okay. You sure?"

Waving a hand dismissively, Tyler forced a laugh. "Yeah. She's like my little sister. Of course, that means I'll beat the crap out of you if you hurt her, though."

Connor raised an eyebrow. "Little sister," he repeated. "I've got a little sister, and I don't give guys the look you just gave me when I said I wanted to ask Bess out."

Crap, was Tyler that obvious?

Cracking a smile, Connor continued, "How about you think it over a bit and get back to me?" He took a couple steps toward him and lowered his voice. "Though if you are interested in her, you better stake your claim fast because there are at least two other guys in this gym who want to be tapping that."

Connor walked away, snickering quietly, probably at the dumbfounded look that Tyler knew he had on his face right now.

Tapping that? Tyler didn't like the idea of any guy saying he wanted to tap Bess Foster. Sweet, maternal, innocent Bess.

As he stalked out of the building, he pictured a few of the guys that Bess might have met at the gym. They weren't all like Connor. More the player-type. Well, hell, if those were the kinds of men that Bess was attracting in those skin tight yoga pants she wore to class, maybe it would be better if Tyler told Connor to go for it.

Connor was a good guy. Stable, too. A part owner in the gym, someone who wouldn't be up and leaving in a year.

Unlike Tyler.

Slamming his car door shut, he blocked out the noise from the busy expressway next to the gym. The sudden quiet around him annoyed him, so he turned on the radio, loud, and let the sounds of Rage Against the Machine pound his eardrums.

Bess and Connor.

Connor and Bess.

The more Tyler heard it in his brain, the more he hated it. He had gotten too used to the idea of the three of them. Tyler, Bess, and Abby. He enjoyed spending time with them. Thinking of another face showing up in their house—*their* house—to whisk Bess off on a date or two made Tyler sick to his stomach.

But he had no right to stand in Connor's way.

Unless he did something about it right now.

Opening the front door of the house, he could see Bess

standing in those damn yoga pants again, the ones that hugged her butt and made him horny as a teenager. Him and all the other guys in the gym, apparently.

"Whatcha making?" he asked innocently.

"Hi. I didn't hear you come in," she said, shooting that smile that always made him feel warm and homey inside. "Just boiling some water for pasta. The boxed kind, this time. Time slipped away from me."

Tyler glanced over at Abby, sitting atop the thick pillow she preferred, rather than the booster seat she now claimed was for babies. "Hi, Tyler. Want pasta? It's the boring kind."

Tyler gulped. Hard. Was he really going to go down this road? "Ugh, no. Not the boring kind. How about I take you out to Horizons instead?" *Horizons*. He almost grimaced at the sound of it. It was the trendiest new restaurant in Annapolis that reeked of "first date."

"Horizons? That place that opened up last winter?" Bess seemed taken aback.

"Yeah. Thought it might be nice to try it."

"Oh, Tyler, that's sweet of you, but it's not really kid-friendly."

Abby frowned. "It doesn't have skeeball?"

Bess laughed. "No, honey. No skeeball. Just a lot of fancy, breakable glasses that aren't really good for chocolate milk."

Abby frowned.

His nerves wavering, Tyler blurted, "We could see if Edith could babysit."

This was met by a squeal of delight from Abby, who preferred going to Edith's house even more than Pirate Pop's Pizza Palace.

Bess stood there, mouth wide open. Tyler approached her, and turned off the stove behind her. "What do you say?"

He would have liked to have seen a hint of pleasure in her eyes at the moment. But all he could see was confusion.

"'Kay," was her only response, slightly breathless, with one side of her face scrunched up in bewilderment.

"Great. I'll call Edith," he said casually.

What am I doing?

What is he doing?

Bess stepped into her room to change, her heart rate skyrocketing, echoing behind the pressure in her ears as her head seemed to swell with blood flow.

Asking her to have dinner with him at Horizons? What was up with that? It wasn't the local pub sort of scene, the kind of place where they'd end up wound into conversations with six people they didn't even know.

No, Horizons was a place for dates, which might explain why Bess had never been there. Eyeing her purse on her dresser, she pulled out her phone and texted—quickly—to Lacey and Maeve. One of them was bound to reply.

"Tyler asked me to dinner at Horizons."

Lacey wrote back first. "WTF? Abby will hate it. Too quiet. Go to Pirate Pop's."

Shoulders sagging, Bess shook her head as she tapped in, "He got Edith to babysit."

Maeve answered next. "Holy !@#$%! That's a DATE, girl. He asked you on a date. Get it????"

Yep, she got it. But still wasn't believing it. "There has to be a different reason."

Lacey piped in. "Hope you shaved your legs this morning," she wrote, adding a smiley face.

Shit! She hadn't! Why would she? No one gets closer than six feet of her bare legs. That makes two days of stubble on her pretty much undetectable.

Maeve wrote, "Sigh. Your silence tells me you didn't."

Then Lacey: "Don't pick on her. She doesn't want to sleep with him on her first date anyway."

She didn't. Did she? Hell, yeah, she did but— "It's not a date," Bess punched in insistently.

"Suuuure," Maeve wrote. "And so you're writing us WHY exactly?" She made a smiley face emoticon—the annoying one with the tongue that stuck out.

Very mature, Maeve. Now Bess was remembering why she hadn't dared to tell her best friends in the world that she had actually kissed Tyler a few days ago. They never would have let up.

"Picking Abby up later anyway," Bess typed in. "Won't happen. What do I wear?"

Lacey wrote first. "Dress you wore to Jack's award ceremony."

Maeve interjected, "No. Too dressy. Tank dress I bought you for your birthday."

Bess wrote back. "He's seen that already. I have a new dress Edith bought me. Kind of form-fitting like the tank dress with spaghetti straps."

"Edith bought you clothes? I love that woman," Maeve wrote. "Strappy is sexy. Go with spaghetti straps."

"But it's kind of tight." Bess resisted.

"All the more reason to wear it," Maeve texted back.

Bess heard a tapping on her door.

"Edith says we can drop Abby off in fifteen minutes. She'll have mac and cheese waiting for her," he finished, followed by a resounding "Yippee!" from Abigail.

"Okay. I'll be out in a minute." *A minute?* It would take her longer than that to get presentable enough for a date.

But this is Tyler, she reminded herself. No matter what Lacey and Maeve said, there had to be some other reason he was taking her out. Maybe he got some good news at work and wanted to celebrate. And she was... available. Like always, come to think of it.

Biting her lip, she pulled the dress over her head, worried that the clinging cotton-spandex blend would reveal too many of her fat folds. She looked in the mirror, holding her breath.

No fat folds, she realized, a feeling of glee washing over her. *How did that happen?*

All those hours on Tyler's treadmill and at the gym seemed to also be having a hell of an impact on her waistline.

Her eyes widened looking at her reflection. And she *had* a waistline, she suddenly realized. For the first time since before she had gotten pregnant, her shape resembled a bit of an hourglass rather than an eggplant.

She reached for the tube of lipstick on her dresser. That, and a touch of mascara might make her look less like an inappropriate companion for a sexy Army Ranger. But she wouldn't put in too much effort. She didn't want Tyler worrying that she had gotten the wrong idea from the invitation.

This was probably a pity date, she decided, giving herself a nod in the mirror. Poor Bess who never gets out. How many times had he told her she should get out more? And now that she had confessed she hadn't kissed a man in four years, she elevated pathetic to a whole new level.

How like him. He was just trying to get her out there again, remind her what it was like to have a date. He had no intentions of actually letting a romance build out of it.

So why the swarm of butterflies in her stomach?

Opening the bedroom door, she was greeted by an exuberant hug from Abby. "Come on, come on!" she said, taking Bess by the hand and dragging her down the stairs. "Mac and cheese," she shouted as she raced out the door to

Tyler's car, with the same enthusiasm as she might have if Bess had just told her they were headed to Disneyworld.

Maybe Bess should really cook Abby more "kid food" than she did. Roasted vegetable ratatouille and beef bourguignon might be a hit with Tyler in this house, but perhaps her daughter should have the chance to experience mac and cheese from time to time.

Bess and Tyler were quiet on the ride over, the air already filled with Abby's excited chatter which ranged in topics from mac and cheese to fairies to unicorns. For a child who took longer than most to finally say her first word a while back, Abby was definitely making up for lost time.

Edith was standing at the doorway waiting for them when they arrived, greeting them both with hugs before taking Abby's hand. "Ready for a slumber party?" Edith asked.

"Slumber party!" Abby responded with glee.

"Oh, no," Bess said quickly. "We'll just pick her up after dinner."

Edith gave a dismissive wave. "Oh, that makes no sense. I have everything she'll need."

"Slumber party! Slumber party!" Abby chanted exuberantly.

Tyler's eyes were as wide as Bess's. "It's no trouble to pick her up. Thanks, though."

"Noooo…" Abby moaned.

Edith shook her head. "It's so much easier on me if you just pick her up in the morning. That way I can go to sleep at the same time Abby does."

"Please, Mama," Abby begged.

Bess felt her palms sweating. "Uh, okay. I guess. You're sure you have everything you'll need?" Bess asked over the delighted squeals from her daughter.

"Dear, she sleeps here all the time during her naps. It's no different." She ushered Abby into her home. "Now you two go have a nice evening," she said, giving a brush of her hand in the air as if to shoo them on their way.

Bess sat back down in the car, watching the smile of the woman waving to them from the doorway. When Tyler turned his head to look behind him as he pulled out, Bess could have sworn Edith sent her a wink.

She was doing this on purpose, Bess was suddenly ready to wager. The only question was whether she had come up with the plan on her own, or had received a call from Lacey or Maeve.

"She's sure good to have around," Tyler said, a hint of awkwardness in his tone.

"Yeah, she's a godsend." She swallowed—hard—wondering how the hell it would feel sleeping in the same house with Tyler without a three-year-old chaperone.

Horizons on the Chesapeake was just outside downtown Annapolis, where the South River opened into the Bay. The massive structure used to be a boatyard that was nearly washed away when Hurricane Isabel hit the region over a decade ago. The decrepit building remained overlooked until about a year ago when it was bought, gutted, and restored to its former glory, housing a restaurant that opened to rave reviews.

Inside was a magnificent view of the Chesapeake from its dining room, and a smattering of antique furnishings that preserved Annapolis's maritime culture.

The entire region was buzzing about it, it seemed to Tyler, from all the articles that he had found on the web about it. Apparently, Annapolis was a town that relished its history and when a lost relic like an old boatyard was restored, it was sufficient cause to celebrate.

It was, as Tyler had predicted, completely packed.

"Looks like there's a wait," Bess noted. "Why don't we just go to a pub or something? There's always a seat at O'Toole's."

No, Tyler thought. O'Tooles was a place he'd go with Bess as a friend.

He'd given himself this one night to figure out if there was something between them or not. With a decent guy like Connor waiting in the wings, it wouldn't be fair to string Bess along. And he sure as hell was more comfortable with the idea of Connor in Bess and Abby's life than some of the other gym rats that were probably scoping out Bess.

"I made a reservation," he said, lightly touching Bess's back as he guided her forward, and gave his name to the hostess. She led them to a table for two set alongside a floor-to-ceiling window. The table was candlelit, with a flame flickering inside a hand-blown glass votive holder. White tablecloths set the tone for a more formal environment than the Annapolis norm, yet the rustic antiques scattered throughout the dining room seemed to lend a balance to the room, making it more comfortable and less stark than it might have been.

Tyler quickly pulled Bess's chair out for her as she sat— something, he'd admit, he generally forgot to do with women. He wasn't exactly raised in a highbrow kind of world in his little hometown in upstate New York. But a guy can pick up a few gentlemanly tricks after being stationed in Savannah, a city that oozes southern charm.

"How did you manage a reservation here on such short notice?" Bess asked.

"I read on the *Post* website that the guy who restored this place was former Special Ops. While you were upstairs changing, I thought I'd take my chances and give him a call—

tell him I'm a Ranger and see if he'd take pity on me." He looked out the window at the view. "Guess it worked. This view is phenomenal."

The hostess handed them their menus. Certainly not the plastic-covered kind that they would have encountered at O'Toole's. In fact, the top of the menu was personalized with their names. "Welcome, Bess and Tyler," it read on the thick paper stock set inside a cloth-covered folder.

Impressive. He'd never seen that before, which might say something about the kind of places where he usually hung out. And it was definitely not the kind of place he would have expected to be opened up by a former Green Beret and his wife.

As Bess stared down at her menu, Tyler drank in her image. She was beautiful—seriously gorgeous—in the candlelight. The light reflected on her red curls, just bright enough that Tyler could still make out the adorable freckles that were scattered from her cheeks to her ears.

"So," Tyler began, feeling fifty shades of awkward ogling a woman he had thought of for so long as sort of a sister-like, off-limits friend, and mother of a child he adored.

There was nothing motherly or sisterly about the way that dress fit her, hugging her breasts so tight, yet without looking like she was putting it all on display. How could something be so sexy and modest at the same time? It made his mind wander to that morning when he had seen her, soaking wet in a white t-shirt.

Damn. They hadn't even ordered drinks yet and he was already sporting a quarter-chub.

"Do you want a bottle of wine?" he finally asked.

"A glass will be more than enough for me."

He'd never admit it, but he was grateful to hear that. He hated wine, much preferring a beer straight out of the bottle. Glancing around, he hoped this wasn't the kind of place that poured beer into a glass. Spotting a beer bottle sitting lone on a nearby table, he heaved a sigh of relief. Of course. This was Annapolis. Beer in a glass was sacrilege here.

"All right," he said, reading the menu. "How about some appetizers to start?"

"No. I really don't need an appetizer."

He could tell she was holding back.

"I know you don't *need*. But do you *want*?" He smiled. "Besides, I'm ordering some. It's not exactly the kind of place I go to often, so I'm living it up. How about calamari? And these lobster and shrimp rolls sound good." He glanced up at her from his menu. "But you're the chef. You'd know what to order better than me."

Bess bit her lip, and gazed down at the menu. "Well, I've never seen parmesan encrusted snapper listed as an appetizer before. I'd love to taste that."

"Perfect," Tyler responded. "I definitely brought the right person here. I'll enjoy it a lot more with you than anyone else."

The look she sent him was questioning, and he could imagine why. Just don't ask, he wanted to tell her. *I have no clue what I'm doing right now.*

A man in a tailored suit came to their table, rather than the waitress Tyler was expecting.

"1st Ranger Battalion?" the man asked.

Tyler nodded.

"Twelve years in 7th Group." The man extended his hand.

Tyler grinned, happy for the distraction from Bess in that dress, and shook his hand. "Tyler Griffon. You must be Major Kincaid, Sir."

"I'm just Lewis now," the man laughed.

"Good to meet you, Sir," Tyler replied, still feeling the urge to address him properly. Rangers were more formal, and Tyler still wore their cultural trappings, even though he might be living in a Navy town for the moment. "This is Bess Foster," he said, giving a nod to Bess, uncertain how exactly to define her. Fortunately there was no need.

"Ms. Foster," he said, greeting her.

"Bess, please," she smiled at him.

"Thanks so much for squeezing us in tonight," Tyler said. "This has to be the best table in the place."

"Anything for fellow Special Ops. Are you still out of Savannah?"

"No, they sent me to the 704th MI Brigade to work on some issues we're facing."

"I'll bet. We're facing plenty, aren't we? How long are you here for?"

"A year at most. Depends on how things evolve. You know the deal."

Lewis nodded. "I remember it well. Don't make plans too far in the future."

"Do you miss being in the action?"

"Not a damn bit. Pardon my language, Ma'am," he directed to Bess. "My wife is pregnant with our second child right now. That's all the action I can take."

"Congratulations," Bess exclaimed. "How old is your first child?"

"She's three in December. My wife wanted kids exactly three years apart, and it looks like she's going to get exactly what she wants."

"My daughter's three, too," Bess said. "Is she in preschool yet?"

"No, we'll probably start that next year." He reached into his pocket and pulled out his iPhone. "Now you're gonna have to indulge me. I'm a pretty proud dad." He pulled up a few photos and handed the phone over to Bess.

"Oh, she's adorable. She has your eyes. I'm a bad mom. I don't have any pictures on me."

"I do," Tyler volunteered, pulling out his phone. "This one's my favorite. Abby at her last birthday. Check out the frosting on her face."

Lewis laughed. "So, obviously she loves chocolate."

"Actually, I'm thinking she would have preferred vanilla, seeing as the frosting ended up *on* her rather than *in* her." Tyler took back his phone. "So, a restaurant? How'd you end up doing that?"

"Actually, my idea was to fix this place up and just sell it. I used to work on houses when I was in between missions. Restoring them. Kind of a hobby of mine. But then when this place started looking good, I teamed up with a couple partners and opened the restaurant."

They talked a while longer, and Lewis said he'd send over a couple extra appetizers he wanted Bess's opinion on after Tyler had volunteered her culinary expertise.

"And if you ever decide you want to work regularly in a kitchen, I'd love to see what you can do. Just give me a call," he said, handing her a card.

"Thanks so much, Lewis. I really appreciate that." Her face was practically glowing as he walked away.

Tyler grinned. "See? I said you were destined to be working in that industry. Apparently, I'm right."

Self-consciously, Bess glanced down at the table. "Oh, he just offered because you talked me up so much. I'm really not as good as you say I am."

Tyler shook his head. "You always underestimate yourself. I'm telling you, if you opened a restaurant, people would flock to it. The stuff you whip up is so—I don't know—inventive."

"Inventive. I like that. Thanks."

"I'm serious. Those baked goods you're always sending in with me to work? You've already got a fan base at Meade from it. And your dinners?" Tyler shook his head. "It's no wonder I'm coming home earlier from work than I ever have in my life." Though looking at Bess now in the candlelight, Tyler caught himself wondering if it was just the food he'd been rushing home to all this time.

Bess smirked. "Anyone can cook with a little practice."

"You're underselling yourself again. I've seen you work in the kitchen and I never see you open a cookbook."

"Oh, I do sometimes. But I guess even then I do kind of like to put my own spin on things."

"If you opened up a little place outside of Hunter Army Airfield down south, you'd be making three meals a day for every Ranger in the Battalion."

Bess shrugged. "It takes a ton of time and a ton of money. Two things I don't have. Besides, I'd really like to learn more about cooking first. There's so much I don't know."

"There are some culinary schools in Baltimore and DC, you know."

Bess smiled. "Yes, and there's a little girl waiting for me at Edith's right now who needs food, housing, and a good insurance plan."

Tyler's shoulders slumped. She was right. A single mom couldn't afford to drop everything and pursue her dreams.

Bess glanced around her, looking upward toward the massive beams the crowned the structure. "I remember driving by this place when it was all run down. I just figured they'd plow it down one day. I never imagined anyone would do something like this with it."

"Yeah, a hell of a change from life in the Green Berets, huh?"

Bess nodded. "Have you ever thought about what you might want to do after the Rangers?"

"Not much. It's still too early to think about getting out. I always figured I'd go to twenty." *Till recently.* His eyes wandered, deep in thought.

Bess seemed to pick up on it. She was always good at that. "You still feel that way?"

"Sometimes. But not always." He pressed his lips together, reaching for his beer. "Rangers can get pretty banged up on missions, and it can make a guy wonder how many good years he's got left, you know? I'll keep doing it as long as I can, but it's not one of those jobs you can do half-assed. Lives are on the line."

"Anything interest you outside of the Rangers?"

You mean other than you? He seriously wanted to ask her. The way the candlelight reflected in her eyes made her look like she should be painted in oil.

Or rubbed down in oil at the very least, he thought, suppressing a smirk.

"Not really," he answered, grateful when the waitress set some appetizers in front of them. Something to focus on other than how tempting Bess looked tonight.

Bess pressed her lips together thoughtfully. "Can I ask you something?"

"Of course."

"You said something to Lewis about staying here a year at most, depending on how things go. What did you mean by that?"

"Well, you never really know about Special Ops. I'm working on some intelligence issues now, and... well, let's just say that if it goes the way we think it might, it will be the basis for a mission. If that happens, I'll have to get back down there fast and deploy."

Breaking eye contact, Bess reached for her wine, concern creasing her forehead.

"Hey, but don't worry. I won't stick you without rent for those months. I'll make sure you're covered for my full lease," he assured her.

Tilting her head, her eyes narrowed. "That's hardly what I'm worried about, Tyler."

He touched her hand, the feel of her skin against his palm warming him from his fingers all the way to the core of his heart. "No need to worry about me, either." He knew the words were somehow lacking. With close friends married to the military, she knew what was at stake.

By the time the entrees arrived, they had sampled six full plates of appetizers and covered just as many topics. Conversation with Bess was as easy in this setting as it was at the kitchen table back at the house, except for the way he felt his heart rate pick up a notch every time she brushed a lock of hair behind her ear. The subtle move was so innocuous, but for some reason it made half the blood in Tyler's brain surge downward.

As the waitress set their entrees in front of them, Tyler suppressed the urge to take a picture of them before he devoured his meal. They looked more like works of art than food.

The owner might be a snake eater—what Army guys called Green Berets—but he sure had a knack for recruiting culinary talent.

"You see, Tyler? This is what I'm talking about. Look at the plating skills." Bess had an appreciative grin as she gazed at her meal. "This is the kind of thing I dream about doing one day. And I'm hell and gone from being this good."

"You have the talent."

"Even if I did, I need the education. Funny how my Bachelor of Arts didn't really prepare me to do something like this," she said, giving a nod to her dish. She flaked off a bite of her salmon, grilled to perfection, and touched it lightly to the sauce that made a delicate pattern over her plate. Her eyes shut as she touched the bite to her lips, and as she chewed, a quiet moan escaped her. "Ohhhh, Tyler, you really have to try this." Opening her eyes, she sliced off a bite for him and brought the fork over toward him.

He took the bite in his mouth. "That's incredible. If you'll cook that up for me, I'll put you through culinary school myself," he said with a laugh.

Taking a forkful of his Macadamia encrusted Mahi Mahi, he sampled his entree. His eyes slammed shut at the taste of the delicate fish layered with a light sweetness from a mango salsa. "You've got to try this," he said, taking another forkful and holding it out to her. As her lips enclosed around the fork, he couldn't help recalling how she had tasted during their brief kiss. Sweeter even than the pineapple mango salsa that was topping his fish.

An air of complete satisfaction on her face, she looked flat-out erotic as she murmured her compliments to the chef.

"Incredible, isn't it?" he said. "Hard to believe the owner's backstory. He must have been pretty ticked off three times a day, sitting down to an MRE. No wonder he got out early."

"That's delicious. Can I have another bite?" she asked, scooting her chair closer to his.

"Sure," he replied, wondering if he should just scoop a portion onto her plate. Yet he loved the intimacy of it— feeding her, feeling the pressure of her mouth against his fork as she pulled the food from it with her mouth. He couldn't resist offering her another bite. "Tastes just like Hawaii to me."

"You've been to Hawaii?"

"When I was enlisted before West Point, I was stationed at Schofield Barracks on Oahu for a couple years. That's when I took up paddleboarding. I tried surfing a few times, but I stunk at it," he said with a laugh.

"Oh, I bet you weren't that bad." She offered him another bite of her salmon. "That's where Vi is going on her honeymoon."

"Oahu?" He took the bite from her fork, savoring the brief connection between them. This was the way to eat dinner, he decided, alternately feeding and being fed by a desirable woman.

"No. Different island. Kauai. Some remote resort right on the beach."

"Kauai's supposed to be beautiful."

"You never went there when you lived there?"

Tyler shook his head as he held out a bite to her. "Not on a Specialist's salary. I stuck pretty much to Oahu. But I still loved it."

Bess pressed her lips together and tossed her head to the side with a slight shrug. "Sounds nice, but Hawaii's kind of down on my to-do list."

Tyler's eyebrows lifted as she closed her mouth around his fork. He had never met a woman who hadn't drooled over the idea of Hawaii. And in the Army, Schofield Barracks was a coveted PCS. "Really? Where would you have chosen for a honeymoon?"

Bess, her mouth still full, smiled a moment as she chewed. "You'll laugh," she finally said.

"I won't. Promise."

"Alaska," she confessed, filling her fork with some of the new potatoes on her plate.

"Alaska," he repeated. "Why would I laugh at that? I hear Alaska is gorgeous in the summer."

Bess's mouth twitched upward into a half-grin, her expression unconsciously sexy to Tyler, as her eyes danced mischievously. "Because I want to go in the winter."

Tyler's chin dropped an inch. "You must love snow."

"Actually, it has nothing to do with the snow. I want to see the Aurora Borealis. You know, the Northern Lights?"

"Really?" he said. Bess was always full of surprises. "Actually, that sounds like a hell of a good place for a honeymoon."

Her eyes rested on him appreciatively. "That's what I thought. Vi looked at me like I was crazy when I suggested it to her. And Lacey and Maeve pretty much took her side."

"They're dead wrong. Any guy would agree with you." Tyler speared some asparagus with his fork. "Think about it. It'd be too cold to even get out of your hotel room much, and that could only be a good thing on a honeymoon, right? Besides, a honeymoon should be a dream destination. If seeing the Northern Lights is a dream of yours, then by God, that's where you should go."

An image popped into Tyler's mind as he chewed on the tender asparagus tips—of Bess snuggled up in a ski parka, standing out on the porch of a resort with a hot spiced wine held tight in the clutch of her mittens, watching one of the most spectacular light displays in the natural world.

Fort Wainwright was just outside of Fairbanks, Alaska. Guys he knew who had been stationed there had always talked about being able to see the aurora borealis. Bet Bess wouldn't mind a year up there with Abby, being able to get her fill of the lightshow with her daughter at her side.

A knot formed in his stomach. And where the hell had that idea come from? He was just on their first date, and already was planning a PCS with her. Better put the brakes on that train of thought.

"Care for dessert?" The waitress asked them, snapping him back to the moment.

Tyler ordered two desserts, not because they were still hungry, but because he didn't want the evening to end. He would have been content to spend the entire night spoon-feeding Bess, even though he could actually think of a few other activities he'd prefer to do with her.

As the desserts disappeared from their plates, Tyler watched her scoop the last spoonful of a custard-filled dessert crepe into her mouth.

"Oh, I can't get enough of this, Tyler," she said, clearly savoring the bite, oblivious that Tyler was imagining her saying the same words in a very different situation.

Okay, so this could be damn awkward at the close of the night, he suddenly realized. He needed to tread carefully here. She was his housemate, he reminded himself. His friend. The mother of the three-year-old Tyler loved fiercely.

Shit. The three-year-old who was away for the whole night at Edith's. That could make things way too tempting.

After he handed his credit card to the waitress, Bess shifted in her seat awkwardly. "I really wish you'd let me chip in. This meal must have cost a fortune."

"No way. And it was worth every penny. I read about this place a couple weeks ago online. I was kind of curious what kind of place a former Green Beret would open up. I needed the company."

"Tyler, look in the mirror. You could have gone with anyone."

"Maybe. But I wanted to go with you." Didn't she see the attraction he felt for her? "Besides, I need to get you out more. You work way too hard. Then you come home and cook for me and Abby."

Bess laughed. "Used to. Now I work out at the gym and feed my kid food from a can."

"That chicken piccata you whipped up the other night sure didn't come from a can."

She waved a hand in his direction. "Oh, that's amateur stuff. Some night I'll make you my smoked trout soufflé. That takes some practice and I actually got it down pretty well. But I'll have to do it on a Saturday. I'm getting pretty used to my weekday workouts at the gym."

Tyler signed the credit card receipt and handed it back to the waitress. "I'm just glad you're enjoying it there. I thought you might. It's good to do something out of your comfort zone every once in a while." *Like taking your housemate out on a date.*

"Yeah. Connor was saying they're starting a women's boxing class. Said I should try it. He said I have a knack for the heavy bag and might really enjoy it."

I'll bet he did. "Boxing, huh? I better behave around you from now on." *And Connor better behave, too.* "Think you'll do it?"

"I guess so. I like the instructor already, and that's half of it. Makes classes a lot less intimidating."

"Who's teaching it?"

"Connor."

Connor again. Standing, he pulled her chair out for her. *Does she have a thing for Connor?*

Feeling suddenly uneasy, he furrowed his brow as they walked out of the restaurant. "So, you like him?"

Bess shrugged as she stepped through the door, her hair catching a breeze off the Bay. "More than the guy who teaches grappling. He scares the hell out of me."

Vlad, Tyler thought. "Yeah, Vlad kind of scares the crap out of everyone." Funny, it was good-natured Connor who Tyler was more concerned about right now, though.

Maybe Bess was hoping Connor would ask her out. And here Tyler had all but put a stop to it.

What kind of a prick did that make Tyler? Bess deserved to be with any guy she wanted, and if she thought Connor was it, then on principle alone, Tyler couldn't stand in the way.

His friendship with Bess suddenly eclipsed his need to whisk her out of sight from any other man who might show an interest in her. "Yeah, I think Connor's got a little thing for you, actually."

Bess stopped dead in her tracks. "Huh?"

"Yeah. He, uh, kind of told me he might like to ask you out sometime."

Her face contorted into—what was that expression exactly? Displeasure? Annoyance? But then the expression faded and she started walking toward the car again. "That's nice, I guess. He's—" she paused. "He's a good guy. He's always really nice to Abby when she goes into child care."

Suddenly feeling suspicious, he frowned. *Totally using the cute kid to get to the mom. Oldest trick in the book.* Tyler might have been buying presents for Abby since the day she was born, but that was completely different. At the time, he'd had no interest in Bess other than friendship.

At the time.

"So you, uh, might be interested in him?" *Ugh.* He suddenly felt like he was back in high school, asking a girl on behalf of his friend whether or not she was interested in him. *So, Bess, Connor wants to go out with you. Do you think he's cute?* He had refused to play that game even back then. And here he was, doing it at 27 years old.

"I guess so," she answered, sliding into his car after he opened her door for her. "Like you said, I really do need to get out more."

Tyler nodded, thoroughly pissed at himself for saying anything.

Would it really have been so bad to stand between them, at least for a little while, to see where this thing was headed?

CHAPTER 11

"It WAS a pity date," Bess had typed into her phone earlier that night, the first moment she was alone in her bedroom.

"What makes you think that?" Lacey had responded first, followed by a nearly identical text from Maeve barely a second after.

"He told me I needed to get out more, then said some guy at the gym, Connor, wanted to ask me out. Doesn't sound like the actions of a man who wanted to get laid tonight, does it?"

There had been a long pause, probably as her friends let reality sink in. Maeve had chimed in first after that. "So, what's Connor look like?"

Bess had laughed a little at Maeve's response at the time. But right now, after three hours of lying awake in her bed, it didn't seem funny at all.

She couldn't let this get to her. Connor was a hell of a consolation prize, and if he actually did ask her out, he'd go down in her history as the hottest man she had ever dated.

Except for Tyler. Because she really *had* thought that the dinner at Horizons had been a date till that moment he'd mentioned Connor. As they had sat there feeding each other, their chairs pulled so close together, Bess had glanced around noticing they looked like the happiest couple in the restaurant.

Happy, maybe. But a couple? Not.

Guess the attraction she thought she had detected in his eyes was more aimed at the food than at her.

Finally giving in to the insomnia, she rose from her bed. Looking at the clock, her mouth curved downward. It was just past two in the morning. Oh, she'd be in a hell of a good mood when she picked up Abby from Edith's house later today.

But she wouldn't worry about that right now. She had time to kill, and what better way to do it than baking? Now that she was spending so much time at the gym, the stand mixer on the counter was actually starting to collect dust.

Stepping quietly past Tyler's door—of course he was probably sleeping like a baby, the son of a bitch—she went downstairs. Flipping on the kitchen light, the glare caused her eyes to burn momentarily. That was her own fault. She had let a few tears drop that night, silly as it all was.

Lacey had been right, way back when Tyler first moved in. It was unhealthy, living with the man she had literally fantasized about for nearly four years. Uncomfortable and awkward, especially when all the feelings she had for him were clearly not reciprocated.

She wanted him, dammit. And here she was now, with her daughter actually away from her for the first night in her life, and Bess didn't have any better way to spend her time than by making some homemade bread for Abby's sandwiches this week.

How could she have fooled herself even for one moment tonight into believing that Tyler might be interested in her? Into thinking that maybe, just maybe, she'd get to actually...

She shuddered, her mind wandering to the bed she always, invariably, slept in alone. Best to not even consider where she had hoped the evening would have ended up.

It's not like Lacey or Maeve would have advised her not to go for it. Really, if she were to end her sexual drought, there was no better person to do it with than Tyler.

But he wasn't interested in her that way. Filling a measuring cup with water, she glanced at her reflection in the window above the sink. It was pitch black outside, and with the light on, Bess could even make out the tear that was streaking down her cheek.

Dammit. She had fallen in love with him. That was the crux of it. The thought didn't even surprise her. She had fallen for him a long time ago. But what was surprising was that she had ever dared to think he might have cared a little for her.

She was just Bess. Frumpy, single mom Bess. Sure she could throw on a little dress bought by her seventy-something-year-old friend (and really, that was just pathetic in itself). But at the core, she was still the girl in the tight ponytail wearing old t-shirts from the clearance rack, working in a job she had no interest in whatsoever.

As the water spilled over the measuring cup, Bess stared at herself in the window as her tears continued to fall, till she saw Tyler's face in the reflection joining hers.

"Bess?" he said, touching her shoulder. "What are you doing up?"

She quickly lowered her gaze to the measuring cup again, wiping her face. "Couldn't sleep. Thought I'd bake some bread for Abby for her lunches."

"Why can't you sleep?"

Still with her back to him, she gave her shoulders a little toss upwards. "Who knows? Haven't been without Abby in the house ever. That might be it."

"I'm sure she's fine. Edith would have called if there were any kind of problem."

Bess nodded, still unable to face him, fearing there might be residual moisture left on her face. There was no way she'd let him know how upset she was. She had to keep some measure of dignity. She poured the water into the bowl and moved to the cabinet to get the bread flour. "Go back to sleep, Tyler. Sorry I woke you. I didn't think I made any noise."

"I couldn't sleep either."

"Really?"

"Yeah. Maybe I'm used to Abby being around, too." He laughed. "Here. Let me get that."

He reached in front of her to get the container, and saw her face for the first time. And from his reaction, she'd have to guess she still looked like she had been crying.

"Bess, what's wrong?"

"Nothing, Tyler. Really." Just shut up, she kept thinking. *And stop being so damn nice to me.* She was too overly tired to keep it all bottled up much longer.

"Abby's really fine, you know."

"I know. It's not Abby." *It's you. It's me.* It's us, she wanted to say. But instead, she moved to another cabinet to look for yeast.

"Then what is it?"

She tossed the yeast packet onto the counter. Now she was angry. He just had to push things, didn't he? "It's you, Tyler. There. You want to know what was making me cry? You."

Tyler looked baffled. "Okay, so now I'm at a loss. Did I do something wrong at dinner or something? I thought you had a good time."

Bess darted a look at him before she turned her eyes back to the stack of measuring cups in front of her. "Oh sure. I'm just a great *buddy* to hang with." She spat out the word "buddy" with as much disdain as she could muster.

"Um, yeah."

"But I'm not good enough to date, am I? Nope. Oh, Bess, she's a good friend, but I'd probably retch if I had to actually end our date with more than a kiss on the cheek and a pat on the head. Better to pass her off to Connor. Maybe he'll take the poor girl out a bit."

Tyler took two steps backward, his brow furrowing. "*That's* what this is about? You wanted tonight to be a date?"

"Yes," Bess hissed, angrily filling up a measuring cup with flour and tempted to toss it in his face. "I'm sorry, Tyler, and this might completely ruin the remainder of your lease here, but I've had a crush on you for four years. Four stupid, pathetic years. And now here I am, living under the same roof with you, knowing that I'm not good enough for a guy like you."

He grabbed her by the shoulders with enough force that she actually felt frightened. "Don't you dare ever say you're not good enough for anyone. You—you're..." His voice trailed a moment as he just stared at her, until suddenly, he crushed his lips against her.

With his lips still joined to hers, she gasped, dropping the measuring cup of flour to the floor in a giant cloud of white dust. His fingers burrowed into her hair as his mouth opened to her. She could feel his breath enter her in heated gasps, as his tongue intermingled with hers. Her arms fell limp to her sides, and her knees buckled just as his arms wrapped around her waist and tugged her closer, supporting her.

Through the thin fabric of her nightgown she could feel his bare chest against her. Her nipples hardened in response. Finally, she resumed control of her extremities, locking her hands behind his neck and eagerly kissing him back.

She was dreaming, after all. She figured she might as well enjoy it.

His hands moved down her back, cupping her bottom, bringing her full against him so that she could feel his erection pressing against her core.

Oh, God. He felt too real, too hard to be a fabrication in a dream. But what other explanation could there be? Reality never felt this good, this erotic. And it was past two in the morning. She was probably face down on the kitchen table right now, passed out from exhaustion.

His hands ventured, touching her breasts so lightly at first she thought she'd have to beg for more of the sensation. No need, she realized as he gripped them fully, toying with her nipples with the pads of his thumbs. One hand moved downward again, slipping underneath her nightshirt, so that she could finally feel his bare hand caressing her like she had imagined so many times. She inhaled sharply when he reached her breast, the touch heightening her awareness of every nerve ending in her body.

She was covered in goosebumps, aching for him to knead every inch of her skin with his hands to warm her body. Lips still joined with hers, his hands slid across her and she felt his body respond fully, so hard beneath his boxers.

He pulled his lips from her. "Oh, God, Bess."

Dizzy suddenly, her eyes were wide with wonder. "So, this really was a date? Tonight, I mean."

"Hell, yes. I just started thinking that you might be interested in Connor. I didn't want to stand in your way."

"How could I possibly think about Connor when you've been all I've wanted for so long?"

A smile crept across his face, and he pulled his torso a few inches from her, still keeping his lower half pressed against her. "I have to take this slow with you."

"You don't," she quickly corrected him.

"I *do*, Bess. You're too special."

Feeling bold, and beyond a little desperate, she reached downward and touched him. He was achingly hard—*for her*, which she still found implausible—and all she wanted was to feel him inside her. "Tyler, I've waited four years to have sex again. And you're telling me I have to wait more?"

He might have laughed, but she was being dead serious. If he sent her back to her bedroom alone, she'd expire. She gripped him, and hope settled in as she watched his eyes slam shut in response. "Please," she implored. "Please do this for me. I need to feel you inside me." She felt her eyes welling up. The need was that all-consuming. That desperate.

Lifting her off the ground easily, he pressed another kiss to her lips, gently this time, so gently it made her heart ache. "In my room," he said as he carried her up the stairs.

Having seen her fill of his muscles before, it shouldn't have surprised her to know he could ascend the stairs so easily with her in his arms. She felt light and airy and so unbelievably feminine from the gesture. Reaching his bed, he lowered her to it gently. "Are you sure, Bess?"

"Tyler, I've never been so sure of anything in my life."

He lowered his body on top of hers, kissing her lightly, so tenderly it made the tiny hairs on her arms stand on end as her body came alive. His mouth traced downward to her neck, and his hands moved to her breasts, feeling their fullness through the fabric of her nightshirt. His eyes locked on hers, as his hand journeyed lower.

"You're so beautiful, Bess," he said, the words themselves acting as some kind of aphrodisiac. Never had a man looked at her with as much sincerity while he had uttered those words. She felt his hand slip beneath her panties, and she arched her body instinctively. So long, too long, since she had felt anything close to resembling this passion.

His fingers moved toward her opening, where she was

moist and oh-so-ready. His thumb found her clit, dying for his touch, and he obliged, tracing the nub in tiny circles as his finger slipped easily inside her. Instinctively, she found herself pressing up against his hand, wanting more and more pressure—never enough. Another finger slipped inside of her, stretching her, moving in and out in a rhythm she craved.

He didn't kiss her now, only leaned back slightly to watch her react as she climbed up on the wave of a climax. So high, she thought she couldn't climb higher. But then his thumb would change its path and his fingers would plunge deeper, and she discovered there were still greater heights looming just out of reach. Her pulse was thundering in her ears, till she finally cried out, quivering, squeezing the last ounce of passion from her core as she felt herself toppling from the heavens back into bed.

His grin was easy. "You're gorgeous when you come," he said, sliding his hand beneath her nightshirt and reaching her breasts. "But you're gorgeous all the time." His lips kissed her face again, tracing her jawline to her ear. "Your eyes have always been my favorite feature. So blue." Kissing her cheekbones, he lifted her nightshirt and brushed his hands across both her breasts. "Though they have some competition now," he added with a grin, moving his mouth downward, taking a nipple into his mouth. She whimpered at the feel of his tongue and teeth teasing her on one breast while his hand explored the other.

Every nerve in her body was firing, every cell springing to life under his touch. Her breaths came quickly—too quickly, making her lightheaded. She felt restless with desire, needing to be closer to him. Only one thing would get him close enough for her desire to be quenched. With a sense of urgency, she pulled her nightshirt off and felt the chill of the air against her skin. Her back arched, lifting her breasts closer to him as he took her back in his mouth.

"More." The demand slipped from her mouth without thought. More of his gentle caresses. More pressure against her. More of his skin gliding against her body. Her list of needs was left unspoken except for that one word, yet he seemed to know exactly what she desired from him.

His chest brushed against her skin as he moved, grabbing the sides of her panties and slipping them off. She felt exposed now, and so vulnerable. She had never had much confidence in the look of her naked body, preferring to not even look at herself in the mirror before stepping into the shower. And in the years since Abby's birth, her confidence had only gotten worse. Sure she might have shed a few pounds these past few weeks, but she still had plenty more acreage of skin than she wanted.

But as he grabbed her hips and his lips caressed her belly, he only smiled. "God, I love your curves, Bess. Do you have any idea how hot you look to me?"

"No," she all but squeaked as he bent her legs, separating them, leaving her feeling even more exposed to his eyes.

"Every time you wear those damn yoga pants, I've wanted to strip them off you and bury myself inside you." He laughed as he went down on her, and the vibration of his laughter tickled her in the most sinful way. Then his tongue plunged inside her, devouring her, making her cry out in sweet, sweet agony. His mouth journeyed up to the center of her arousal, toying with her lightly as he moved his fingers in and out of her, making her mad with desire. She rocked her body against him, writhing, his fingers not nearly reaching as deep as she wanted him.

It was impossible for this to be enough for her... she thought. But just as the thought ventured into her mind, the pressure built inside her again, her body coiling from the need to explode, till the spasms shook her, uncontrollable, pleasure bursting from her in sharp cries.

"Tyler," she repeated his name—she had no idea how many times, till her body again sank boneless into his mattress.

She settled her fingers onto his shoulders as his face met hers. For so long she had wanted to touch him like this, dig her hands into his corded back, stroke forward to that impossibly rigid six-pack. And now she could. She savored the moment, soaking in the feel of his flesh beneath her hands.

"Now," she said, her hand reaching for him, tracing along the ridge of his arousal. "I need you now." She slipped her hand beneath his boxers and purred at the feel of the hot, thin skin sheathing something so hard. Pulsating beneath her touch, he tore off his boxers and her eyes suddenly widened.

"Oh, God, please tell me you have a condom, Tyler. It probably goes without saying that I don't have any."

"I do," he said, his brow arching suddenly. "I think. I— unpacked them. Put them somewhere." Panic touched his features.

Lifting himself off her, she could see his naked form fully for the first time, a body that could inspire a Greek myth.

"Shit. I wasn't expecting this tonight," he admitted.

"Oh, no." Biting her lip uneasily, her entire body wanted to revolt—or race out the door to the nearest drugstore.

He searched through his nightstand drawer, dumping its contents on the floor. "Not in here." Frustration building in his eyes, he shook his head. "Of course. I didn't expect to bring a woman back to the house with Abby living here. Where they hell did I put them?"

He raced over to his dresser, dumping about ten pairs of tightly balled up socks on the floor. "Found them!" he cried triumphantly, then tossing his body back on the bed. He tore open the wrapper and slipped it on. "Okay, after all that excitement, what do I have to do to get you back in the mood?" His hand moved in between her legs, and feeling the moisture, he smiled. "Nothing, I see."

Bess laughed. No, nothing at all. Just watching his hard, broad form tearing through his drawers and darting across the room was a show she could happily watch every day. He was adorable. Sexy. Even in a state of panic, he was everything she'd ever dreamed about in a man.

And she had certainly spent plenty of time dreaming about Tyler.

He lowered himself alongside her, his hand gliding down her breasts, her belly, till he finally rested it on her hip. "You're sure about this Bess? I know it's been a long time. I don't want to push you. I can just hold you all night." A half grin sidled up his face. "I'll be taking a hell of a cold shower in the morning, but I'll live."

"I'm sure," she said, a hint of anxiety edging into her heart. "Please don't have second thoughts."

He moved on top of her, bracing his weight with his arms at either side of her. "Not on your life."

She parted her legs and felt the pressure of him against her opening. She was nervous suddenly, feeling almost virgin-like in her fears. It had been so long. And she had never had sex after becoming a mother. Would it feel different? Would she feel different to him?

The fear must have shown in her eyes. "It's okay, Bess," he assured her, lowering his hips as he began to enter her. "It's okay, baby." His eyes shut for a few moments as he slid inside of her—not too deep at first, as though he was just testing the waters. He opened his eyes and watched her for a response. "Are you okay, beautiful?"

It was such a sensation. Her entire mind, body, and soul felt overwhelmed. Unable to speak, she just nodded. He edged his way deeper inside of her, then pulling out slightly, before pressing into her folds again. "You feel so good, Bess," he said, his voice strained and husky.

His words soothed her, knowing that it felt as good to him as it did to her. Each time he moved his hips, he pressed a little deeper, a little harder, and pausing after each movement to gauge her reaction.

Moaning slightly as he pulsated inside of her, her eyelids were half shut, and she watched him beneath a canopy of her lashes.

Nothing had ever felt so exquisite. So tender, yet so erotic, his movements inside her made her hotter, wetter, and more ready to be completely filled by him. Lifting her hips, she met his next thrust, and a hunger washed over his face.

"Bess..." His voice trailed just as his control seemed to shatter. He plunged harder now, his own need setting the rhythm, and she cried out when he slammed against her innermost depth, pressing up against a profoundly sensitive place that had her suddenly bucking beneath him.

The orgasm consumed her instantly, hard and relentless, seeming to come out of nowhere. There was no slow climb up this wave, only a fierce free-fall that had her heart slamming behind her ribcage and her breath caught in her throat.

Her body seized up around him, the moist folds seeming to pull him in even more, till her soul crashed back into her body, giving her breath once more.

Gasping for air, she purred with him still inside her. "I don't know where that one came from."

"I have some idea," he responded, moving her to her side, easing her leg up against his hip. He was still so hard inside her, but seemed to want her to recover. "Slow and steady for a little while," he said, moving in and out of her, achingly unhurried. His hands caressed her, covering every square inch of her skin within his reach, paying particular attention to her breasts which felt swollen and alive with sensation.

As he moved inside her again, her eyes moved downward, watching the place where they were joined. She wanted all her senses to stay alert of the moment, soaking in his scents, his feel, and yes, even his taste as she moved to his mouth to explore him with her tongue.

Gently, he moved her onto her back again. "So beautiful," he said.

Bracing himself on one arm, his hand moved to her hair as it spilled across the pillow. He opened his mouth as if to say something, but held back.

"What?" she asked, just as his rhythm picked up pace.

Giving a patient smile, he slowed again. "Nothing." Then he shook his head. "I'm just wondering how I could have known you for four years without really seeing you this way, Bess. You are… a goddess."

To that, she laughed but couldn't argue with him since he pressed his mouth against hers to silence her. He pushed himself deep inside her, the friction of where their bodies were joined casting a fire over her, heating her again from her core to the very ends of her fingertips. In and out he thrust, setting a rhythm based on raw need now. No patience. No control. She luxuriated in it, watching his muscles tighten beneath his skin. Sensation pooled inside her again, forcing her higher and higher on a wave each time he thrust. She was trembling, panting in synchrony with him, and the moans that escaped her were only drowned out by his own.

When his eyes shut and jaw clenched, she could feel the moment when she knew he was at his breaking point. She joined him in the ecstasy, her hips reaching up to him with urgency just as he finally shattered inside her. Her own

climax burst forth from her, leaving her shuddering beneath him.

In unison, their bodies breathed heavily as he moved to her side.

Thoroughly satiated, she smiled as she traced the ridges of his arm upward to his face, and her touch was greeted by his warm smile.

"So I have an important question for you, Bess."

If she weren't completely exhausted, she would have felt nervous from the seriousness of his tone. "What's that?"

"Just how often do you get a case of insomnia like this?"

She laughed, her hand reaching behind his neck and pulling his face closer to hers. "Often."

"I was hoping you'd say that." Grinning, he met his lips to hers.

CHAPTER 12

Tyler awakened on his side, opening his eyes to the sight of Bess lying beside him. Her mouth was slightly open and her bare chest gently rose and fell as she breathed.

She was a hell of a sight in the morning, having the same effect on him as watching the sun rise over Diamond Head in Hawaii. He'd have to take her there one day, he decided. Abby would love watching pods of dolphins skimming along the shoreline or whales breaching from the water, even viewable from the beaches.

Bess murmured something, and Tyler watched her, gauging whether she was starting to awaken or whether she was just talking in her sleep.

Still out like a light, he surmised, feeling slightly disappointed. They had a little more time before they'd need to pick up Abby, and there was one way Tyler would love to spend his morning.

The sunbeam that had awakened him, peeking in between the two shades, was slowly making its way toward Bess. He slipped from his bed to close the blinds as best he could. He wished he had some blackout shades right now. But seeing as he usually had to wake up in the pre-dawn hours for PT, there had never been a need before.

Pulling on his shorts, he noticed his room was messier than he would have preferred for company. He hadn't exactly expected to be entertaining a guest, he thought with a satisfied smirk. Not that he was complaining. But he'd definitely tidy up in here later.

He reached for a t-shirt. Then, thinking the better of it, set it back down in the drawer. She seemed to like him barechested and he was sure as hell going to need everything working to his advantage this morning.

Stealing a glance at Bess again, his lips pressed together in thought. It wasn't going to be an easy morning. That much he knew. But he was tough enough to survive it.

Slipping from his room, he decided to make breakfast for her. She was always cooking for him. Time to turn the tables. Even if he couldn't impress her with his skills in the kitchen, it might be enough to throw her off balance, make her waiver a little bit, give him just enough time to make a few salient points in the argument they were about to have. She'd call it a "discussion," most likely. But it would definitely be an argument.

Bess was going to have regrets.

He sure as hell didn't.

After filling the coffeemaker, he opened the kitchen cabinets. He could make pancakes, maybe. *Damn.* Pancake mix was nowhere to be found. *Of course not.* Bess would make something like that from scratch. If he had thought to grab his iPhone or his laptop from his room before he left, he might have looked up a recipe online. But there was no way he was going to possibly wake Bess just to get something from his room.

Giving the fridge door a tug, he spotted eggs. *An omelet.*

His wouldn't be nearly as good as hers always were, but it was the effort that counted.

He pulled out a few eggs, and a handful of other ingredients. He had only made scrambled eggs in the past, but had watched Bess do omelets enough that he was confident he could pull this off.

He chopped up some onions first. Then mushrooms, and was pretty damn proud of himself when he remembered to wash them first. What else did she put in there? Cheese, and he'd try a little ham. Who didn't like ham, right?

Finding the whisk in the drawer, he started to stir the eggs. Did the cheese go in first? No, she always sprinkled it on while the omelet was cooking, he was pretty sure, right along with meat and vegetables.

Holding his breath, he poured the eggs into the skillet and felt some measure of satisfaction hearing the same sizzle that he heard when she cooked one up for him. He couldn't be that far off the mark.

"'Morning." Bess's quiet voice had him turning around.

"Damn. You're up already. So much for breakfast in bed."

"Oh, is that for me?"

He nodded, giving his skillet a glance. The sides of the omelet were starting to harden, so he sprinkled on the meat and vegetables, trying to look confident.

"That's really nice of you," she responded. Her voice was weary, and there was no doubt why. He had allowed her only an hour of sleep last night, having enjoyed a couple more rounds of lovemaking after the first.

After so much time spent in the field, he functioned pretty well after a sleepless night, especially if he was having the adrenaline rush that came from being in a firefight. And facing Bess this morning was a pretty damn close equivalent.

"I'm sorry about last night," she said quietly.

As expected. He frowned, more because his omelet wasn't

143

quite looking right than because of her words. Her statement was right on schedule.

"You're sorry? That doesn't say much about my performance, now, does it?" He winked, pulling a spatula from the drawer. "I'll have to try a little harder next time."

"That's not what I meant."

"I know," he said, trying to ease up the sides of the omelet to give it a flip. "I know what you meant. Right now, you're thinking about Abby. About whether things will change now, and how? And how will it affect her. I know you, Bess, and I know exactly what you're thinking. That's why I'm cooking you breakfast."

"Why?"

"Because I was hoping I'd be able to stuff something in your mouth so I wouldn't have to hear it. You got up earlier than I thought you would."

"So you're stuck hearing it now. Because it's the truth. I totally made the wrong move, Tyler. I was being so selfish."

"Selfish? No, I don't remember you being at all selfish last night," he said, cracking a wide grin.

"I'm trying to be serious here, Tyler. We can't do this again."

Now he was getting pissed... at the omelet. It refused to come free from the pan. "I'll act the same around Abby. She'll never see me groping or ogling her freaking hot mom. But when I get you alone again, all bets are off." His grin faded, giving in. "What the hell is wrong with this damn omelet?"

Standing up, she looked over his shoulder. "Did you melt butter in the pan first?"

"Damn," he said, watching his omelet start to resemble scrambled eggs. "I should have had some coffee before I started this." So much for being good on one hour of sleep.

"It's okay. It'll taste fine," she said, uncertainty in her eyes as he scraped it onto a plate.

He stole a sample bite and shook his head. "No. It's horrible." He must seem tragic to her, he figured, unable to make a simple breakfast. In truth, before he had moved in with Bess and Abby, he had pretty much been a protein bar kind of guy in the morning. "Put on some clothes. I'm taking you out for breakfast."

"Tyler, really. We have to talk this over."

So predictable.

He raised a finger. "Not till you at least drink your coffee. You get a little on the negative side before you've had your morning coffee." He poured her a cup, adding a touch of the sweetened creamer she liked.

Taking the offered mug from his hand, Bess chugged at least half of it in a quick series of gulps. "Okay. Better?"

He nodded.

"You know we can't continue this."

"Continue what exactly?" Tyler asked innocently.

Puzzled, she looked at him for a full ten seconds before answering. "You and me. Having sex in this house. That had to be a one-time thing." She cocked her head at his completely ambivalent look. "I have a three-year-old daughter who lives with us."

"I know. I've met her. And there's this crazy thing called 'babysitters.'"

She dropped her gaze to her mug. "I'm not sending her off to Edith's every time we want to have sex."

"Hell, I'm not saying that either, or I'd never get to see that little girl again. But if you think I'm going to let you tell me that last night meant nothing to you, that we can just go back to being friends, then you're in for a surprise. I'm not a one-night-stand type of guy, Bess. Never have been. And sure won't be with someone I care so much about. So I'm all for pretending that nothing has changed around Abby. She's three. No need to confuse her. But the next time I get you alone, it might take a crowbar to pull me off you."

Having made his point, he gave a nod. "Now, since I've proven you're the only competent chef in the house, we're going out to eat."

"Tyler—" she began.

"Get dressed," he cut her off. "If you're planning on listing any more reasons why last night shouldn't have happened, you're going to have to wait till I have a full stomach."

"Tyler—"

That does it. He picked her up, tossing her body over his shoulder.

"What are you doing? Put me down!" Her tone was half-screech and half-laughter.

"I'm hungry, woman," he said in his most caveman-like tone. "You're getting dressed and we're going out." He carried her up the stairs to her room as she giggled hysterically.

"You're crazy."

"Yep. Crazy for you." He plopped her on her bed and opened her closet. *Geech.* The girl owned more chewed-up t-shirts than even he did. He pulled a blue one from a hanger. "Here," he said, tossing it her way. "Where do you keep your bras? Much as I prefer you without one, I have a feeling you'll want one anyway."

"Left top drawer," she said, her face flushed from laughing so hard.

He tossed her a bra and, finding a pair of sensible white panties in there, which was apparently the only kind she owned, tossed her those as well. "Pants?" he asked.

"Middle drawer. But Tyler, I'm not going out for breakfast. I need to shower. Brush my teeth."

"You won't need to where we're headed." He grinned as he tore off to his own room to put on some clothes. This was a much better idea anyway.

After loading a reluctant Bess into his car, he pulled out of the driveway.

"Where are we headed?"

"Just north of the Academy. I discovered a food truck that has breakfast sandwiches almost as good as your omelets. Almost." He emphasized, flipping on the radio, hopefully to keep her quiet for a while. No sense in listening to her droning on about the supposed mistake they had just made all the way up the coast.

It was a short drive to Dawn's, the low-key food truck planted in a parking lot a block away from a public park that overlooked the Magothy River.

He had read about Dawn's on a local foodie website. It wasn't his normal thing, reading about restaurants, till he had started to imagine Bess opening one some day. Now, he found it all fascinating, reading about how people had broken into the business, where they got their training, or if they even had any.

Dawn, owner of Dawn's food truck, was a single mom, too, older than Bess by a couple decades. When her two sons went to college, she had opened up the food truck to pay for their education. There was no diploma from Le Cordon Bleu Paris on her résumé.

Despite that, business seemed to be booming the couple times Tyler had come up here to eat. A long line stretched across the parking lot.

He shared Dawn's story as they stood in line, hoping to plant a little seed in Bess, start her thinking that maybe her dreams didn't need to be put on the shelf forever. For a brief moment, he could envision her so clearly in the future—opening up a food truck someplace or maybe a full-blown restaurant like Horizons after culinary school.

"I've never eaten at a food truck," Bess admitted, after

being handed three piping hot breakfast sandwiches wrapped in paper. "Who is the third sandwich for?"

"Me. You think one sandwich can hold a guy like me?" he laughed. "Come on, Bess, you know me." He slipped one of his hands around hers, and led her toward a park bench. "Thought we'd grab a seat and eat with a water view."

"Great idea."

Sitting down, he reached into the bag and handed her a sandwich. "Now take one bite of this sandwich and tell me that your omelets couldn't draw just as much of a crowd."

Tentatively, she sank her teeth into the egg and bacon sandwich on a buttered, home-baked English muffin. "This is really good."

"Yeah, I know. But it's nothing compared to your omelets. I mean, don't get me wrong. I think Dawn is a master with these breakfast sandwiches. But Bess," he lowered his voice glancing over his shoulder to the food truck on the other end of the park, "you have to look at that place and know that you could do the same thing *and* do it better. If you opened up a food truck off Meade serving up those omelets of yours, you'd have Soldiers lined up along Reece Road every morning. You could call it 'The Big O' or something."

Bess let a little snort slip as the laughed. "The Big O. Maeve would love that."

"Just something to think about." Chewing his sandwich, he savored the idea of Bess sometime breaking free of that damn dental office to pursue her dream, whether in a food truck or a Zagat-rated restaurant. Hell, he hated going to the dentist. *And she has to do it five times a week?*

Gazing out at the water, he noticed it was a very different scene here than closer into downtown Annapolis. On the Magothy, there were more powerboats than sailboats. Tyler gathered it must be because of the shallower waters of the river. Yet still, it was a lively scene, even at this hour of the morning, with a few people crabbing off docks and a handful of joggers.

Across the river, the houses here were more humble than the sprawling new construction that overlooked much of the Chesapeake Bay. Mostly 1950s ranch houses, more modest and a hell of a lot less intimidating. Spotting a little white ranch with blue shutters and window boxes, his mind wandered. He might be able to afford a place like that one day soon, even on the water, if he looked for a house in this area.

And why the hell was he thinking about the future so much this morning?

He smiled when he felt the tension finally leave her body, as she snuggled a little closer to him on the bench.

"Thanks, Tyler."

"For what?"

"For believing in me." Nibbling her bottom lip, she pulled away about an inch. "Your friendship means so much to me. Too much. And you're so special to Abby." She paused, letting out a long sigh. "Don't you think it would be safer if we just pretended that last night never happened?"

"Probably," he said, draping his arm over her shoulder and pulling her close again. "But if I liked to play things safe, I wouldn't be a Ranger." Having made his point, he lifted her chin upward with his finger and did the only thing he could think of to silence her.

He kissed her. Thoroughly.

Bess pulled her car out of the driveway. Things looked no less confusing to her after a good breakfast and a hot shower.

So, he wanted this to continue. She should be elated

149

about it. Aside from the birth of her little girl, Tyler Griffon was the best thing that had ever happened to her.

But what she'd never dare to admit was that her worries about their relationship reached far beyond concern about its effect on Abby. Bess was worried about herself.

Even if they continued their relationship for the remainder of the time he was here, what would happen when he left? When he moved someplace else and found someone new? If he were anyone else, she'd be able to cut all ties with him.

But he was Tyler, Abby's hero. Her honorary uncle, bearer of a constant stream of gifts. The man who had promised to whisk her away to Disneyworld one day.

Abby needed Tyler in her life. And that meant Bess would have to tolerate hearing from him even after he had moved on to someone else.

When he eventually married, had kids of his own, she'd hear about it. Hell, she wouldn't be surprised if she ended up getting a wedding invitation.

Her phone beeped, alerting her to a text. Seeing as this would likely be her last moment alone for a while before picking up Abby, she pulled off to the side of the road along Spa Creek, where a handful of fishermen were sitting on the docks.

She gazed down at her phone. "Feeling any better?" Lacey had written, followed by, "Men suck," added by Maeve.

Oh, God. Bess groaned inwardly. She should feel a school-girl excitement at the prospect of telling her two best friends in the world that she had just had sex with the man of her dreams. But as it was, she only felt a knot in her stomach.

"Kind of. Just sort of confused now," Bess wrote them back.

It took only a few seconds before Maeve's reply came in first. "Can't believe he led you on like that. Horizons is totally a date place. Doesn't he know that??? I vote you should just ignore him this morning."

"I second that," Lacey typed in next.

Bess shook her head, reading their replies. *Here goes nothing.* "Sort of hard to do," she wrote, "since we just had sex last night."

Her cell phone immediately rang. "What are you talking about?" Maeve's voice rang out the instant Bess answered.

Bess laughed. Obviously Maeve was the faster dialer of her two friends. "We sort of had sex last night."

"Shut the fu… front door," Maeve stuttered, and Bess could picture her sitting at the kitchen table with her two children. Yep, no more foul language out of Maeve unless the kids were asleep.

"Yeah. I was downstairs around 2 a.m. Just couldn't sleep."

"I'll bet."

"And neither could he. So one minute we're talking, and then next—oh, wait, Lacey's calling on the other line."

"Don't you dare stop talking now," Maeve threatened.

"Okay, okay. I'll call her back. Anyway, we're suddenly kissing. Then he picks me up—literally sweeps me off my feet—I could have died. And the next minute I'm in his bed having the best sex I've ever had in my life. Including my fantasy life." The phone beeped again. "Hold on a sec. She'll keep calling till I pick up."

"Tell her you'll call her back. I need the story and we're headed to church in a few minutes. Ha! How ironic is that? Want me to ask for a little absolution for you, Bess?"

Bess groaned in response, switching over to Lacey.

For the next ten minutes, she was bouncing in between two calls, giving her friends the briefest update possible, till Maeve finally had to leave for church with Jack and the kids.

"So are you going to bring him to Vi's wedding in a couple weeks?" Lacey asked.

"I hadn't thought about that. Do you think I should?"

"Of course. Geez, you slept with the guy. He'd probably be hurt if you didn't ask him. Besides, he'll want to see you in that bridesmaid dress."

Bess winced. "I still haven't tried it on yet."

"Are you crazy?"

"Probably. But with that tight bodice, I just keep thinking it won't fit me. Don't tell Vi, okay?"

"I won't. She's stressed enough right now with Joe in Qatar till next Sunday. Keeps thinking he'll be held over in the meetings and will miss his own wedding."

"That won't happen though, right?"

"No. Mick says that it would take something really cataclysmic for them to make him miss his own wedding. He's just TDY, not like he's deployed or something. But she's freaking out anyway. So the last thing she needs to hear is that one of her bridesmaids won't even try on her gown to make sure they sent her the right size."

"I'll try it on. I promise."

"If I were you, I'd be more worried that it might fall right off you. What with all the weight you've been losing. Before you know it, you'll be in better shape than Tyler."

"Ha!" A laugh exploded from Bess. "You've never seen the guy naked. He looks like he stepped out of *Men's Fitness* magazine, except that he's not photoshopped."

Lacey laughed. "Yeah, Special Ops guys have to be in pretty amazing shape. Just watch out. Mick says they soften up after retirement."

"Oh, he'll be long gone by that time, anyway."

Bess heard a sigh from Lacey. "Bess, stop planning on this thing to end already. I know you, and that's what you're doing, aren't you? You're shooting the horse before it even makes it out of the gate."

"No. Well, maybe. I'm just so worried about Abby getting more attached to him."

"You mean that *you'll* get more attached to him."

"Maybe, yeah. Definitely. But even when we break this thing off—"

"—*if* you break this thing off—"

"—I still need to keep him in my life, Lacey. Abby adores him."

"Well, then I suggest you buy some more of those spaghetti strapped dresses that Edith got you and pull out all the stops."

"Yeah. Figures Edith would know just where to shop. The woman's well over seventy and more in tune with today's trends than—Oh my god."

"What?"

"Edith. I'm late picking up Abby. Gotta run."

Edith. She only hoped that Edith didn't want the details of what happened last night like her other friends had demanded.

CHAPTER 13

Freshly showered, Bess sat on her bed, still winded from tonight's grappling class, staring at the strapless chiffon bridesmaid gown as it hung in her closet. It had been over a week since she had promised Lacey she'd try it on.

She could use Tyler as an excuse. He certainly kept her busy anytime they weren't at work or the gym. Taking full advantage of autumn in Annapolis, he had taken them to two corn mazes, three fall festivals, and one hay ride that had Bess's eyes puffing up like melons from allergies. And on the rare rainy days, they tried their hand at duckpin bowling and enjoyed a couple evenings of skeeball at Pirate Pop's.

It was like they were pretending to be a family, and the feeling was becoming a little too addictive for Bess.

And for Abby, she worried.

Laughter and few jubilant squeals from Abby drifted down the hall. After finishing a makeshift dinner of leftovers —with their busy schedule, Bess found less time to cook these days—Tyler had volunteered to put Abby to bed. But she was still "torqued up," as Tyler always put it, from ninety minutes of rambunctious playing in the gym's child care room.

"She's supposed to be winding down now, Tyler," Bess called into the next room. "Quiet time. You know, reading a book or something."

"Nooo…" She heard the whine from Abby, and a few more squeaks of the bed as she jumped on it, followed by Tyler's calm tone, no doubt telling her to pick out a book for him to read.

Bess smiled, imagining them in the room together. They could pass as any father-daughter pair these days, and it warmed Bess's heart, at the same time it was breaking it. How would Abby handle it when Tyler left next year to return to Savannah and the 1st Ranger Battalion? Anytime the two were together in public, little Abby would reach for Tyler's hand as if to tell the world, "He's with me."

Bess knew exactly how her daughter felt.

Barely five feet away, the blue chiffon mocked her again, pulling her mind back to the present and the wedding that was just over a week away. Jack and Maeve would be coming up the Wednesday before the wedding, the first time Bess would see them as parents.

Jack and Maeve. Parents. Bess was excited to meet their kids, and secretly so hopeful that they would get along well with Abby. How horrible would it be if the three children despised each other?

Giving a little shake, she assured herself it wouldn't happen. Marcus was just Abby's age—the perfect playmate. And Kayla, at eight, might serve as a good older sister role model for Abby one day just like Maeve had always been to Bess.

It would be so good to have all her friends together again. That first night when they arrived, Bess planned on making a nice meal for all of them, here in this wonderful house where all of her friends had found their true loves.

Could Bess dare to hope she'd have a happy ending in this house, too?

Well, it certainly wouldn't happen if she couldn't manage to squeeze into that damn dress.

Giving an internal nod, she finally stood, ready to take on the dress and defeat it. With all the exercise she had been getting, it was absurd to think that it would be too small. But after four years of being disappointed by the way things fit her, the idea of putting on the dress could only make her feel just this side of panic.

Reaching out, she took the dress off the hanger. She slipped it over her head and felt the lightweight chiffon drape over her skin.

It seemed… loose.

Seriously loose.

Reaching behind her, she struggled with the zipper. Frowning, she went to her door. "Tyler, can you come in here a sec?"

Within moments, he appeared at her door, his eyebrows lifting an inch at the sight of her *almost* in the dress. "Wow. That's gorgeous."

"Yeah, but I can't get it zipped up. Can you help?"

With a smirk, he approached her.

She narrowed her eyes. "Don't get any fancy ideas. I just can't reach the zipper."

"Likely excuse," he said, coming up behind her. He paused a moment, his hand touching the bare skin of her back only an instant, making her ache for more. Her eyes shut momentarily, her mind drifting into a fantasy of him slipping his hands beneath the chiffon, stroking her back, her sides, and eventually reaching her breasts.

Oh, God, how she missed his touch. Was it driving him

nearly as crazy as it was her? Opening her eyes to gaze at him, she couldn't tell from the reflection of their image in the mirror.

He zipped the dress and looked at her quizzically "It's beautiful on you, but way too big," he commented.

Still needing to hold up the dress in front of her to keep it on, she stared at her image. "Oh my God."

"Don't worry. It's not a big deal to take it in. We'll need to pay for a rush job, but I'm sure we can find someone who will do it."

Her eyes glistened with tears as she soaked in her reflection. How many times had she had the nightmare of putting on clothing that didn't fit, watching her weight spiral out of control right along with her whole life these past years? A tear streaked downward on her cheek.

Tyler came up behind her and put his hands on her shoulders. "Bess, don't get upset. It's really doable. You won't be without a dress for the wedding. I guarantee it. Even if I have to take the damn thing in with duct tape myself."

Bess laughed. Military guys sure liked to fix things with duct tape. "I'm not upset," she said, with a smile. "I'm thrilled." A fit of laughter escaped her. "I'm ecstatic. I was fitted for this gown just before you moved in. It was going to be snug. Now it's falling off of me."

"You've lost a ton of weight since you started working out. And you've firmed up." A playful smile touched his lips. "I know. I felt that muscle tone first-hand. How could you not have noticed?"

Bess shrugged, remembering what Edith had said. "Everything I own has an elastic waistband. I knew I'd lost a little weight but I didn't realize how much. I'm the kind of person who doesn't like to look in mirrors much, Tyler."

Tyler turned her around to face him. Cupping her face gently in his hands, his eyes met hers. "Bess, you've always been beautiful. You might be a bit thinner now, but you've always been beautiful. Don't ever forget that. There's more to beauty than whether or not you can squeeze into a size 6, okay?" He glanced briefly at the door and then stole a kiss, sweet and sensual at the same time. It wasn't nearly enough for her, and Bess ached to dial Edith right now and see if she could watch Abby for the night.

Pulling his face back from hers, Tyler grinned, walking toward the bedroom door. "Abby! Come on in here and check out your pretty mama in her bridesmaid gown."

Abby quickly appeared at the door, with a colorful book in her clutches. "You look like a princess, Mama."

Still holding up the dress, Bess agreed, "I feel like a princess in it. Your Aunt Maeve picked it out."

"Not as pretty as my flower girl dress though," Abby said, swaying back and forth.

"Nothing is as pretty as that. Just remember, though, you're not the only flower girl this year. Your Aunt Maeve's little girl will be one, too."

"No, she's a junior bridesmaid," Abby corrected. "Aunt Maeve said so."

Tyler reached out for a hand from each of them. "And how lucky will I be to have two pretty girls as my dates that night?"

Abby lunged at Tyler's leg, wrapping her arms around it like a boa constrictor. "Let's go back to the story," she said, handing him the book and dragging him by the hand toward the doorway.

Tyler grinned. "My presence is required elsewhere," he said to Bess. "Meet me downstairs after I put her to bed, okay? Just give me a minute. We're on the last page."

Stealing a glance at him as he walked out the door, Bess detected a hint of mischief in his eyes. She sure hoped so, anyway.

Shutting the door, she sighed contentedly. The dress was too big. All these weeks of trying to get stronger had made her thinner in the process. Biting her lip, she pulled off the dress and hung it back in her closet. She'd take it to the seamstress at the mall tomorrow morning, she decided. For a price, they'd certainly be able to do it in time.

She hoped.

Slipping on her comfy yoga pants and a t-shirt, Bess emerged from her room to complete silence. Abby's light was off and Tyler must have gone downstairs already.

"Love you, Mama," Bess heard Abby murmur as she slipped by her door.

Unable to resist her daughter, Bess stepped inside her room a moment, and planted a kiss on her daughter's forehead. "Love you, too, baby. Call me if you need me." Abby's eyes fluttered shut, already drifting to sleep.

Bess watched her a moment, her heart swelling with love. Never once had she taken for granted the miracle of her child in her life. Her perfect little girl—well, perfect to her mama anyway.

She shut Abby's door halfway and went downstairs. The house was dark, and the back door was open. She stepped into the doorway, feeling a warm autumn breeze rolling off the Bay and into the house. Candlelight in the backyard caught her eye, and she stepped outside. After her eyes adjusted, she saw Tyler sitting on a picnic blanket spread out on the lawn.

"What's all this?" she asked moving toward him.

"A dessert picnic. I figured it's all we could manage after Abby was put to bed. I picked up some crème brûlées at that gourmet shop off Main Street." He pulled a cork from a bottle of wine. "And some dessert wine," he added as he poured it into two glasses.

"Tyler, that's so sweet. But Abby—"

"Sound asleep already, I'm betting." Tyler reached behind him and pulled off the remote for the baby monitor he had clipped to his shorts. "But if she stirs, we'll know it." He set it on the grass beside them.

Bess sat on the blanket. "You are so thoughtful."

"Not thoughtful at all. Just desperate to get some time alone with you."

"It's hard with Abby around, isn't it?"

Tyler tossed his shoulders up lightly. "I can't complain. She's fun to be around. But you?" He leaned forward, touching his lips to hers. "You are an entirely different kind of fun. If Abby didn't end up crawling into bed with you half her nights, I might be tempted to do the same." He handed her a glass of wine. "This is a dessert wine Maeve recommended."

"You called Maeve?"

"Actually, I called Lacey first for advice. I'm really clueless when it comes to wine. But she confessed she usually buys wine in a box, so she gave me Maeve's number. Guess she's a wine connoisseur, huh?"

"She is."

He pulled out a propane torch. "So, want to see if these crème brûlées are any good?"

As he lit the two ramekins, the fire blazed, browning the sugar. The glow was alluring, and the sizzling sound made her mouth water just as the smell of vanilla bean wafted past her nose.

"You lit those like a pro," she commented.

"No different than lighting the coals on a Weber." He started to hand her a spoon, but seemed to think the better of it, instead dipping the spoon into the ramekin and scooping out a bite.

Extending it to her, she took it in her mouth, feeling her hormones spike.

"How is it?" he asked.

"You be the judge," she replied, dipping the spoon into his ramekin and feeding him. The way his mouth closed around the spoon made her shiver, remembering how it felt to have those lips toying with her and tasting her. The need to have that kind of satisfaction again burned inside of her.

"It's good," he said, his tone less than enthusiastic. "But not nearly as tasty as you." Careful to not knock over the two votive candles in the grass, he reached for her, caressing a tender path from the cleft in her chin, along her jawline, to the back of her head. He pulled her closer, his mouth meeting hers eagerly, urging hers open for him. Then she tasted him, savoring the saltiness mixed with a hint of vanilla. He was decadent to her, a craving she'd have every day for her lifetime.

With his mouth barely an inch from hers, his breath tickled her lips as he spoke. "I've been dying to get you alone, Bess. But I figured this might be the best we could do for a while."

"I'll take what I can get," Bess murmured in response, her eyes widening briefly when she heard a soft sigh coming from the baby monitor. "You know, I nearly threw that baby monitor out last spring. I thought I had reached the point when I didn't need it anymore."

"I vote we keep it till she's eighteen."

She warmed inside at the idea of him still being around then, even if he had been just joking. "Edith suggested she take Abby to her house after the wedding for the night. Abby will wear out pretty early in the evening and Edith said she'd love an excuse to slip out early, too."

"I love that woman."

"Me, too." Taking another bite of the dessert, she looked up at the stars. "It's funny. I guess it's sort of sad that my family was so unsupportive of Abby and me. But it's such a miracle that I ended up here, you know? Here in this house, with friends who really adopted me as their family. Not many people get so lucky in life."

Tyler cocked his head to the side. "What are your parents like?"

Bess pressed her lips together. She didn't like talking about her parents and always appreciated that Tyler didn't bring it up. But he must be curious, really. What the hell kind of parents would cut their only daughter and granddaughter out of their lives so easily?

"They're—I don't know—very strict. Religious. That fire-and-brimstone type of deal where I walked out of church every Sunday certain that God was going to strike me down with a lightning bolt any minute."

"You were an only child?"

"Mmhmm. My mother told me once they had tried for years to have a second child, but she imagined that God wouldn't let her get pregnant again because I'd need all their attention to keep me from getting into trouble."

"Charming woman," Tyler retorted, dripping with sarcasm.

"Yeah. Doesn't really sound like they had much confidence in me, does it?" Bess stretched out her legs.

"Also sounds like they should have gone to a different church. The only thing the chaplain browbeat us about at West Point was this funny thing called duty. To your family. Your teammates."

"Guess they missed that sermon," she said, pulling in her knees to her chest. She could change the topic now, she considered. But for some reason, she wanted him to know everything. "So anyway, I didn't date much, to say the least. The first guy I dated was in my freshman year of college and wow, that went over like a lead balloon with my parents. My father had a 'talk' with him. Think he scared him to pieces—not like in the violent way because my father, well, he's kind of a slight man. But just in the way that the guy must have thought, 'why even get involved with this totally messed up family?' I can't say I blamed him when he broke up with me the next day. Said I really should find someone who would fit into my family better. I was furious. Not with him, of course. But with my parents. Especially my dad."

She paused, taking a long sip of wine to bolster her courage. "Then my junior year, Dan came along. My dad had the same little talk with him and he didn't scare him away at all. In fact, he seemed to want me even more after that. He wanted to help me break free of my family's hold on me, he told me. And I bought it. But looking back, I think he only wanted to pull me away from them so that he could control me more. When he asked me to move in with him, my parents warned me that he was no good, and pretty much disowned me. And then the abuse started right after that."

Tyler pulled her closer, almost up onto his lap as he let her use his chest as a backrest.

She sighed from the warmth and understanding that enveloped her. "I think one of the reasons I let it continue as long as I did was because I kept thinking I had to make it better. I couldn't let my parents be right about him."

His hand stroked her hair lightly and she melted further into him in response.

"Do you ever think about contacting them again?" he asked.

Bess frowned. "No. Funny, isn't it? I don't have the slightest inclination. When I called them a couple years ago to tell them about Abby and they rejected her, I realized that they have no place in my life. I won't subject my daughter to them. Why would I welcome anyone into her life that doesn't look at her like the jewel she is?"

163

He shifted slightly so that their eyes could meet. "You are an amazing mother, Bess. I hope you know that."

Bess gave a little shrug. "I try."

"No, you don't *try*. You *do*. With your history, I'm not sure how you learned to be a good mother with the parents you had. But you definitely succeeded."

His hand pulled her closer, and he kissed her. The taste of him was like an elixir curing her of the remnants of anger and rejection that festered inside her whenever she spoke of her parents. For four years, Tyler had been the fantasy that gave her hope that there might be a man out there for her. And now, he was the promise that she truly could open her heart to someone completely.

Arching her back toward him, her breasts pressed against his chest as he laid her back on the blanket. He sucked in her lower lip, his teeth lightly scraping against her, stoking the fire that burned low in her belly.

Sliding his body fully on top of her to reach toward the two votive candles, he licked his fingers and pinched out the tiny flames with his fingertips. She winced slightly at the sight—never could understand how anyone could do that.

The darkness engulfed them, making the stars above them appear even brighter. Bess felt emboldened by it, glancing again at tiny green power light of the baby monitor. Surely, Abby was sound asleep. Bess could even hear her gentle breathing through the remote.

Did she dare do this? Her desire consuming her, she felt she had little choice as she gave in to her passion and opened her mouth fully to him, taking him in as deeply as she could. She was lost to her own yearnings now.

He moved his hand low on her belly, slipping under the t-shirt and gliding up toward her breast. She practically purred from the feel of his hands on her. It had been too long since they had made love.

Under the canopy of darkness, he lifted her t-shirt, and took her breast in his mouth. The moan that escaped her was filled with need as a sweet, sinful agony pooled inside her. She pressed her hips upward, demanding pressure from his body, and his hands moved lower in response, slipping beneath the tight waistband of her yoga pants and meeting her warmth. He tunneled his fingers into her curls and found the center of her need, massaging it expertly beneath his fingers. He moved further between her legs, finding her wet and so ready for him. She gasped as his fingers slipped inside the delicate folds. With an aching tenderness, his fingers moved inside her, in and out as he stole her moisture for the hard nub that ached for his touch. Slow and steady, not in a rush at all, his other hand moved to her breast as he toyed with her. He licked her nipple, letting the autumn breeze dry it, and then took her in his mouth again.

A shooting star shot across the sky as she lay beneath him and she gasped from the splintering climax that was within her reach. Higher and higher she soared until finally she saw stars—not the ones that shone down on them from the heavens, but the brighter, piercing kind that radiated from the back of her eyes.

Pressing his mouth to hers, he muffled her cry with his kiss, feeling her quake beneath him till her body melted, pliant, into the blanket.

Still winded from the flood of sensations that had just coursed through her body, she reached for him, wanting to take him to the same level of ecstasy. Just as she reached for the zipper of his shorts, they heard it:

"Mama, I'm thirsty."

Bess's eyes flew open from the voice that called out from the baby monitor, snapping her into a very awkward reality. "Oh, Tyler."

She could barely see his face in the darkness as she heard him utter a soft curse.

"How am I going to survive until Edith takes her after Vi's wedding?" he asked.

Bess grimaced, as she pulled her hand away from the erection that was pressing against his shorts. *Poor guy.* "I'm so sorry, Tyler."

"Don't be. Go get that little girl some water. I'd offer to do it for you, but I'll be indisposed for a while," he said, the tiniest hint of humor making Bess feel a little better. Just a little, as she headed back inside to her wonderful, perfect, *demanding* daughter.

CHAPTER 14

The sun was setting much earlier these days, Tyler noticed as he went inside to turn the porch lights on. A warm glow had settled over the Bay, blanketed in the distance by a gentle mist. Glancing behind him as he flicked the switch, he saw Bess tossing back her head in laughter at something one of her friends had said. Her hair glimmered in the light of the setting sun, pulled up in a loose ponytail, revealing a porcelain neck that begged to be kissed.

Tyler swallowed and looked away. With three officers who outranked him, and the company of three young children, now was definitely not the time to get aroused by Bess in those tempting spaghetti straps that kept flopping off her shoulders.

Mick came up to him as he stepped back onto the porch. "Thanks for having us all over, Tyler."

Tyler shrugged. "No problem, Commander. Bess barely even let me help. She cooked everything herself, even though I offered to order out. This is her thing, though. She totally went Martha Stewart on me this week preparing. She was in her zone."

"You're telling me. She single-handedly catered my entire wedding, you know."

"No kidding, Sir? I never knew that."

"We had hired a caterer who backed out last minute. Bess took care of everything. Everyone said it was the best wedding food they had ever tasted. She'd probably have signed up to do Vi's if there weren't four hundred people coming. The place is going to be a circus."

Tyler's eyes settled on Bess in the distance. "She's got such talent. It kills me to see her wasting away working in a dental office, you know?"

"When you have kids, it's all about putting your own dreams on the back burner sometimes."

Tyler nodded, watching Abby playing with Maeve's two adopted children. They seemed to be engaged in a game of freeze tag. Kayla, the older one, was looking mildly exasperated, trying to get the two three-year-olds to play by the rules. But already, the girl had a patience Tyler admired. He was never that patient at eight years old.

Tyler smiled at the sight. "The kids are getting along great. I know Bess is relieved about that."

"They'll grow up thinking of each other as family," Jack said as he approached, handing them both a fresh bottle of Sam Adams. The gesture was friendly, but his eyes on Tyler were just this side of lethal. "The way we all do. Bess is like a sister to Mick and me."

Tyler knew what Jack was insinuating. "I'm aware of that, Sir. Bess is grateful for the family."

Jack sat down on the porch step, tossing back a quick sip of the beer he held in his hand. "She seems pretty fond of you these days."

Mick rolled his eyes. "Heel, Cujo. Take it easy on him. Tyler's a good guy, Jack."

Tyler sat on the step near Jack. If he was going to have

this conversation, he might as well be sitting down for it. "No worries, Commander. If Lieutenant Commander Falcone has something to say to me, he's welcome to say it."

"Well, in that case, I'll leave you two alone." Chuckling softly, Mick made his way across the lawn and joined in a conversation with Vi and Joe.

Gazing out to the Bay, Jack didn't meet Tyler's eyes. "Mick told me what you did for Bess. Facing down that bastard ex of hers. I want you to know I appreciate it."

Okay, so this wasn't what Tyler was expecting. He cocked his head, waiting for the "but."

Jack pressed his lips together. "I wish I had been here to help."

"You're in Little Creek, Sir."

"Just the same, it's not too far to drive if the need arises. So keep that in mind. If something else happens and you need back up. I'll want to be notified. I won't be at sea anytime soon and can be up here in a matter of hours. Do you think we've seen the last of him?"

"Wish to God I could say for sure."

"Well, you can count on me. Captain Shey, too," he added, tossing a nod in Joe's direction. "He's intimidating as hell, but that could only work to our benefit."

Tyler laughed, feeling slightly more at ease.

"All that aside—" Jack began.

Here it comes.

"—I'm not sure I approve of you leveling up the relationship with Bess."

Well, that's a diplomatic way of putting it.

"And your reasoning, Sir?"

"I grew up with four sisters. I've seen the way that women get attached, and then get their hearts broken. Bess has enough on her plate right now. Raising a kid. She doesn't need to deal with that when you move on to someone else."

"*When* I move on, Sir? Don't you mean *if*?"

"You're an Army guy living in a Navy town. You won't be growing roots here in Annapolis, and you know it."

"Meade's a big base. I could spend the better portion of my career stationed there if I wanted to."

"But you won't. You're a Ranger. You'll head back to your Battalion. You won't break ties with the brotherhood over some girl you fell for in Annapolis, no matter how great a cook she is."

Tyler narrowed his gaze on Jack. "May I speak freely, Sir?"

"Please do."

"Maybe you're not around here enough to know this, but Bess is a damn sight better than just 'some girl' a guy falls for in Annapolis. And you don't know what's in the future for us any more than you knew with your own wife when your relationship started. But I'm sure as hell not going to be intimidated by you or Commander Riley, or even Captain Shey when it comes to my relationship with Bess."

Jack cracked a smile. "Bess is a grown woman. She's free to date anyone she wants without our approval. But I won't take kindly to it if you lead her on, *Lieutenant*."

"I'm getting promoted to Captain next month."

"Congratulations. Isn't that one pretty automatic?" Apparently, Jack couldn't resist a dig.

"I've asked Bess and Abby to put my bars on me."

From the way his expression changed, the significance wasn't lost to Jack. At promotion ceremonies, it was customary for the officer to ask someone close to him to attach his new rank to his uniform in front of the audience. Usually the honor went to a wife or parent. In the absence of those two at the ceremony, a mentoring commander usually filled in.

It generally wasn't a task handed to a girlfriend, unless

the Soldier had intentions of making her a permanent feature in his life.

Bess had been happy to accept the invitation to do it. But being a civilian, she hadn't really known the significance of her and Abby being a part of the ceremony.

Slowly, Jack nodded, his features softening slightly. "Good," he said. "If you're smart, you'll make sure she's still around for the next promotion ceremony, too." As he stood, he gave Tyler a swift thump on the shoulder that Tyler could only interpret as a gesture of acceptance into their clan.

Even if he was the lowest man on the totem pole here, it was a good place to be.

Across the lawn from him, Bess glanced over as Jack walked away. She smiled, and came to sit beside Tyler. "Are you having an okay time?"

"Better than okay. The dinner was fantastic."

She eyed Jack suspiciously in the distance. "Jack wasn't giving you a hard time or anything, was he? He's kind of protective, and he doesn't know you as well as Mick does."

"He's fine. Don't worry. A lieutenant commander isn't about to scare me away." He lowered his voice. "But if Captain Shey starts in on me, I might need to call for reinforcements. You know he's pretty much a SEAL legend."

Bess giggled softly, watching the Captain on all fours giving pony rides to Abby and Maeve's children on his back, while Vi snapped a photo of her fiancé on her phone and threatened to put it on her Facebook page.

He certainly didn't look much like a hardened SEAL commander at the moment.

A sigh escaped Bess. "They're so in love, Tyler. It's nice to see. They look like they were meant to be." She leaned into him slightly, and he fought the urge to drape his arm around her. He had promised to keep his hands to himself around

Abby, but the more time they spent together, the more difficult he was finding the task.

"You're a romantic."

"I am, and proud of it." Bess grinned. "I'm so excited for their wedding now that I know I can actually manage to get in my dress."

"I'm more excited about getting you *out* of the dress." He snuck a brief touch of his hand to her back. "Edith is still fine with babysitting afterward?" He glanced over at the older woman who was sitting out on the dock talking to Lacey.

"Yep. I just double-checked a few minutes ago. She's looking forward to it."

Tyler's smile was wide. "Not as much as I am."

With Bess catapulted into a million last-minute wedding plans, Tyler barely got to see her over the next few days.

So by the time the Naval Academy Chapel was filled, with Joe eagerly waiting at the front for the arrival of his bride, Tyler was feeling just as much anticipation waiting for one of the bridesmaids to walk down the aisle.

Edith was sitting next to him in the pew, and she patted his knee reassuringly. "As nervous as you look, Tyler, I'd be guessing that you're the groom."

"Just hoping she and Abby are doing okay back there." They had been whisked away from him and into the bridal room when they arrived, Bess looking radiant in her form-fitting dress and Abby like the perfect angel in white. Tyler barely had time to say good-bye. "Abby was getting a little crabby from all the excitement. I wish I could help back there."

Edith laughed. "You would definitely not be welcome in the bridal room."

"Yeah, what's the mystery there, anyway, Mrs. B? What is it they do in there?"

Edith's expression warmed. "Oh, a lot of laughter, a lot of tears, and probably a little champagne to take the edge off."

"Sounds like what happens with the groomsmen then, minus the tears." Tyler had been in his fair share of weddings, but certainly not any as huge as this one was. The chapel was packed, and Bess told him they had needed to rent out two adjoining hotel ballrooms for the reception just to accommodate the crowd. "I really hope Abby doesn't get overwhelmed. That's a long aisle she has to walk down. And a lot of distractions along the way."

"Don't worry. Bess will be walking in before her, so she'll be at the other end waiting for her."

"Maybe I should—"

"It'll be fine, Tyler." Tilting her head, she gazed at him. "You really love that little girl, don't you?"

"With all my heart," he confessed, barely even realizing he had said it out loud before glancing over his shoulder again, staring at the massive double doors that led to chapel.

"And Bess?" Edith grinned. "You'll forgive me for asking, of course. We old ladies like to speak our mind."

As he looked at the chapel doors, a memory flashed in his mind, so sharp it could have been yesterday. A vision of Bess, pregnant, standing in the doorway wrapping her coat around her to shield herself from the chill. He had first met Bess here, four years ago.

How would he have known then that the woman he had just met would bring so much meaning to his life?

"We met here, you know," Tyler finally began to answer. "Commander Riley had been giving Lacey, Maeve, and Bess a tour of the Academy when I bumped into them. She was pregnant then. I assumed she was married, so didn't really give her a second look. Then for the next four years, I wonder if I ever really *saw* her until just recently. I was always so focused on Abby, and Bess was always rushing around, making sure everyone else was taken care of. Does anyone ever really look at her?" It was a metaphorical question, of course, and he was surprised he had even asked it aloud. But it was the truth. There was so much to Bess. So many layers of beauty inside her. And it had taken four years to even reach past the first layer.

Just then the sound violins flowed over the crowd, hushing the guests to silence. The music was Bach, though Tyler would never admit he knew it. Having a sister who had played cello for fourteen years, he had heard his share of Bach growing up.

Joe's parents walked down the aisle first, then Vi's parents.

Then, he saw her and his heart stopped.

Bess.

Looking luminous, her hair swooped into a chignon and her face as perfect as porcelain doll, she stepped into the aisle. The dress was stunning, fitting her new figure and looking like it had literally been designed just for her lovely curves. The bodice was nipped in at the waist and chiffon flowed downward to the floor making it seem as though she was literally walking on air.

"She's beautiful," he barely whispered, more to himself than anyone else.

Their eyes met immediately, which Tyler thought was a miracle in this crowd, but the pull between them was impossible to deny. He felt it, as sure as he felt his heart rate quickening in his chest.

He saw her in that moment. Really saw her. Not as a mother. Not as a friend. Only as a woman. A woman he loved.

That shouldn't actually be a surprise to him. How

couldn't he love her? How couldn't he love the woman who had brought Abby into the world?

But this was different, he realized. He was *in* love with her.

As she passed his pew, it was all he could do not to reach out to her, just to reassure himself that she was real.

That this feeling was real.

A string of other bridesmaids followed, none holding a candle to how gorgeous his Bess looked. His Bess, he confirmed, feeling proud to be the one who got to go home with her that night. Lacey entered last as the Maid of Honor. She sent him a playful wink as she passed, till she joined her friends at the front of the aisle.

Maeve's daughter came next, the little girl looking especially proud in her junior bridesmaid dress. She joined her little brother who stood next to the groom as the ring bearer at the front of the aisle.

How complete Maeve and Jack's family was now. One minute, they were still barely shaking off their newlywed status. The next, they were a family of four.

Abby appeared next at the start of the aisle and Tyler held his breath as she walked toward the altar in her billowing white flower girl dress carrying a bouquet. She gave him a wave as she approached him, and he felt his chest burst with pride from her acknowledgement.

One day, she'd be the bride, he suddenly realized. Her first three years of life had gone by so quickly. He could imagine turning around one day, and seeing Abby as a young woman. Suddenly, wanting to be there for all the moments in between now and then, he felt his palms sweating.

He stood as the bride arrived. Vi looked spectacular, and Tyler glanced quickly to the groom that awaited her at the end of the aisle. It was kind of funny, seeing a tough SEAL

CO look like the wind had just been knocked out of him by the sight of his bride approaching.

Tyler cracked a smile and whispered to Edith, "He's got it bad for her, doesn't he?"

"Head over heels," she concurred.

Tyler knew how he felt.

CHAPTER 15

Bess's eyes fluttered open to a sight she would never tire of. Tyler lay next to her in a solid slumber. Obviously she had exhausted the poor guy the night before. How could she not? An overnight babysitter wasn't a common occurrence and she had to make the best use of the time she had alone with him.

Glancing at the clock, she calculated how much time they had left together alone. She could probably postpone picking up Abby till after breakfast. Edith wouldn't mind. And Abby was never anxious to leave her Grandma Edie's.

She should feel exhausted right now. But somehow, she felt exhilarated. Last night had been magical, as though Vi and Joe's wedding had been ripped from the pages of a fairy tale. The reception was practically a star-studded affair by Annapolis's standards. There were at least three Admirals present, and a ton of newscasters and on-air financial analysts. Even Bess had recognized a lot of their faces from TV, and she tended to watch more *Sesame Street* than anything else these days.

Lazily stretching, she weighed the possibility of getting

out of bed and making some coffee. She imagined they both would need some ASAP before they'd be up to anything else.

Careful not to let the floorboards squeak beneath her feet, she slipped on her panties and padded over to his dresser to pull out one of his PT shirts. Sure, she could just go to her room and get her own t-shirt, but she had always heard men found it a turn-on when women wore their clothes. And that could only work to her benefit, considering what she'd like to do with him after he got out of bed.

Tiptoeing downstairs, she noticed how quiet everything seemed. How strange it was to not have Abby in the house. She felt a little tug at her heart, missing her girl, even after only being apart a matter of hours. Watching Abby walk down that aisle as a flower girl had made her so proud.

Flicking on the kitchen light, the sight of the Bay through the kitchen window beckoned her near. She answered the call, opening the door to the back porch and stepping outside. The sounds of the Chesapeake greeted her with waves lapping against the dock, and a seagull crying in the distance.

The morning sun cast its light on a sugar maple in the back yard showcasing its blazing red leaves, signaling the peak of autumn colors in Maryland. It was the tree planted by Maeve and Jack at the party they had thrown to celebrate their marriage, not twenty feet from the crepe myrtle Lacey and Mick had planted on their wedding night to symbolize their growing love.

In a couple weeks, when Joe and Vi returned from their honeymoon, they'd plant a tree in this yard, too. An oak, Vi had chosen, calling it "a solid investment tree with slow but steady growth potential."

Cracking a smile at the thought, Bess went back inside.

Pouring water into the coffeemaker, she listened to it

sizzle in response, sort of the same way her blood sizzled every time Tyler came close.

Like now. Even with her back turned, she could feel his presence in the room even before he touched her.

He slid his hands around her waist and touched his lips to her neck. "How did I manage to let you slip out of my bed?" he pondered in between the kisses that he planted along a path from her neck up to her ear.

"You were out like a light."

"Well, I'm not anymore." He rubbed a specific part of him against her. "No, I'm wide awake. Every part of me."

She purred in response, feeling arousal building inside of her. Coffee before anything, was her usual mantra. But right now, she didn't quite feel the need for anything but him.

Turning to him, her breasts brushed against his bare chest, making her nipples tighten into hard nubs from the sensation, even through his PT shirt. Apparently, he noticed, easing his hands underneath the shirt and taking them both in his grasp. "Do you have any idea how I suffered at that reception last night?"

"What do you mean?" she asked, her voice breathless as he moved the shirt upward and sucked on a breast.

He removed his mouth, letting the moisture he left on her nipple evaporate under his warm breath as he spoke. "Watching you all night in that dress. Dancing so close to you without being able to toss you on one of those tables and have my way with you."

"Yeah, that probably wouldn't have gone over well."

She felt the hard ridge of him beneath his PT shorts that hung low on his waist revealing a six-pack and tight V of muscles that disappeared below the elastic. Unable to resist, her hand moved there, slipping beneath the waistband and finding him ready for her.

He sucked in a breath as she gripped him. "Yeah," he said,

his voice husky. "When you slipped into the ladies' room, I was seriously tempted to follow you in and lock the door behind me."

"Oh, really? And what would you have done to me in there? Laid me down on the hard floor?" She teased, not about to mention that there had actually been a comfortable sofa in the powder room, and Bess had been sorely tempted to invite him in there herself.

"I wouldn't need to get you horizontal to make you come for me." He growled low in her ear as he turned her around so that her back was toward him and dipped his hand inside her panties.

"You certainly boast a lot, Ranger. But I hear you Soldiers are all talk, no action."

"Is that what your Navy friends are telling you, Ma'am? Well, it's my duty to set you straight," he responded, bending her slightly at the waist, as his finger slipped inside her moisture. She gripped the counter in front of her, instinctively leaning forward to allow him to move deeper inside her.

"Take me upstairs, Tyler," she demanded.

"Oh, no," he answered, pulling her panties down. "I'll take you right here. You presented me with a challenge." From the corner of her eye, she watched him pull a condom from his shorts' pocket and unwrap it. He only pulled his shorts down halfway before sheathing himself. "Open your legs for me, Bess." His voice was raw with need as he kissed the tender skin at the top of her spine. She did as she was told, feeling his hands gripping her hips, molding her into the form he needed. She ached for his penetration, till she felt her wet folds yielding to him as he slid inside her.

Her breath caught from the sensation, the angle of his arousal inside her while standing something new and unexpected. She could feel the tip of him pounding against her womb with each thrust and she cried out.

"You okay, baby?" his voice crackled as his hands reached around to her front and fondled the center of her need. "I'm not hurting you, am I?"

She bent lower over the counter, wanting him even deeper. "No. You feel amazing."

His mouth was against her neck again and she could feel him smile. He shifted slightly, thrusting harder as he did. "Tell me if it's too much, baby."

"No, don't stop." *Please, don't stop.* Whatever you do, don't stop, the voice in her head demanded as she felt the climax taking hold of her, wrapping its sensual claws around her, gripping her tight till she could barely breathe.

Pulling his hand away from her clit, she nearly screamed from its departure. But then he licked his fingers and brought the moisture back down to her.

"You feel so good, Bess," he murmured as his fingers toyed with her, and he thrust harder. Her body rocked against the counter as he moved inside her.

"Don't stop. Oh, please. I'm so close," she begged and his fingers quickened their massage in response. He was so deep, so hard, and yet still she wanted more, bending further over the granite counter. Feeling as though her consciousness was rising outside of herself momentarily, a wave of dizziness overtook her as her body quaked. The fire pooled at her center, till the spasms crushed inside her, making her tighten up around him even harder. She cried out from her own body's eruption of desire, just as he shattered along with her.

Breathing hard, he wrapped his arms around her protectively.

"Oh my," she whispered, feeling him slide out from her.

"You okay, there?"

"Mmmm," was all she could respond.

Still leaning over the counter, she could hear him pull off the condom and toss it in the trash, then pulling his shorts back up. "Come here," he said, lifting her into his arms. "You look like you might collapse."

He took her to the couch in the living room and stretched her out. Shaking his head momentarily, his gaze on her naked form made her shiver.

"You're beautiful, Bess," he said, easing himself over her to kiss her as his hands slid across her body. "Do you know that?"

Bess smirked, gazing up at him. "I'm not entirely sure. Care to convince me further?"

He grinned as his lips met hers, giving a playful nip. "Coffee first?"

She feigned a look of disappointment. "I guess, if you need recovery time," she said, reaching down for him. She toyed with him lightly, uncertain whether her touch would even be welcome before he was able to recover.

His arousal began to build in her hand, and he grinned at her.

"Damn, Bess. How do you do that to me? Maybe I can skip the coffee," he said, then crushing his mouth against hers.

CHAPTER 16

It was almost scary to Bess how comfortable things had become after Vi's wedding was behind them, and Maeve, Jack, and their kids had returned to Little Creek. Lacey and Mick were back in DC, and Joe and Vi had taken off on their honeymoon, so life in Annapolis had fallen into an easy, comfortable routine for Bess, Tyler, and Abby.

The weeks were filled with work, the gym, and plenty of dinners out at Abby's favorite kid-friendly restaurants. On the weekends, they were rarely in the house, always headed out to DC to explore the ample selection of Smithsonian museums.

Coming home one evening, Bess glanced behind her at Abby dozing in her car seat. Her daughter was flourishing with all the outings and attention. Bess couldn't help wonder how she'd ever manage to keep up this pace after Tyler left next summer.

The sun dipped below the horizon just as they pulled into the driveway. Tyler scooped Abby into his arms and carried her into the house.

Bess would never tire of it—seeing this man holding her little girl.

After settling Abby into her bed and shutting the door, she walked back downstairs. The phone rang and Bess picked it up before even looking at the caller ID so that it wouldn't wake Abby.

"Hello?"

"Well, Bess, looks like you've found yourself some rich friends. Haven't you?"

Bess paled at the voice on the other end. *Dan.*

"First I find out you're living in some waterfront house. And now I see those wedding pictures of you with your rich, famous friends online. You and your little girl." He paused. "Or should I say *our* little girl? She has my eyes, don't you think? Wonder if that boyfriend of yours noticed that? Wouldn't that mess up your pretty little life there if he found out? I'm not so sure I'll keep my mouth shut about that."

Fury surged inside of Bess, and her fist clenched around the phone.

She wasn't the Bess Dan had knocked around four years ago. She wouldn't cower. She wouldn't quake in fear. Not any more. Her voice was low and deliberate. "You listen to me, you son of a bitch, if you come anywhere near my girl, I will blow a hole in you the size of Montana."

It must have not been the response he had expected, because the phone went dead on the other end.

Her body vibrating, Bess stood frozen, balancing her weight against the kitchen counter as Tyler walked into the room.

"Who was that on the phone?"

She couldn't reply for a moment, still gathering her wits about her. He came up behind her and touched his hand to her back. "Bess?"

"It was Dan," she finally said. "He knows about Abby. He

saw some pictures online of the wedding." She shook her head. "Dammit. I should have known this would happen with so much press there. I just thought they couldn't print pictures of a minor without some kind of consent from me."

"I don't think they can. But one of the guests probably posted something on their damn Facebook page. It's impossible keeping anything off the web these days."

Panic ripped through Bess. "What am I going to do? What if he wants some kind of custody of Abby?"

"I won't let it happen. Understand? The guy's got a police record. No way they'd pass Abby off to him after you put it on record that he beat you. Besides, if he even tried to get some kind of DNA proof, I doubt he'd have much luck. I've got someone I know in JAG. He should be able to help. We'll call him tomorrow morning." He pulled her over to a kitchen chair and sat her down. "Tell me exactly what he said."

It was a blur, recalling his exact words even though the conversation was so brief. It had been hard to hear him over the pounding in her brain at the sound of his voice. "Umm, he just said something about me hanging out with rich friends. And that he saw Abby's photo. And something like, 'what if your boyfriend found out she's mine?' and how that would mess up my life. That's the best I can remember."

Tyler leaned back in his chair. "Well, shit. He's not even after Abby. He wants money."

"What?"

"Yeah. Shut-up money. Think about it. Did he say anything about wanting her? Wanting to meet her? The only thing he did say was basically a threat to tell your boyfriend. He thinks *I* think Abby is mine. He wants money from you to keep him from telling me otherwise." He scoffed. "It's the only thing that makes sense. You think a guy like him wants to pay child support?"

Bess stared at him. "No. No, I guess not. I don't know, though."

Tyler's eyes were daggers. "Well, there's one way to find out. I've got some calls to make."

Crossing his arms, Tyler eased back on the hood of the sports car and waited for Dan to come to the parking lot. Glancing at his watch, he noted it was seventeen hundred hours. Dan didn't strike him as the type to work overtime, so his wait shouldn't be too long.

The internet, for all its failings, was at least helpful in finding the location of Dan's employer, which was conveniently located in a half-vacated office building. Not many people around to notice a guy in an Army uniform sitting comfortably on the hood of a Lotus.

Just fifteen minutes later, Dan exited the building, casually at first, oblivious to Tyler's presence as a hood ornament on his car. When he spotted him, he picked up his pace. "Hey!" he shouted. "What the fuck are you doing sitting on my car?"

Tyler peeled off his sunglasses, and saw the moment when Dan recognized him as the man who had plastered his fist against his face. Tyler gave his head a little shake. The fool should have known he'd be paying him a visit after contacting Bess.

Dan squared his shoulders as he approached, probably trying to look bigger than he was. Failed at that, too, Tyler noted.

"I said, get the fuck off my car," Dan shouted, looking to both his sides, obviously with the hope someone might be a witness.

"*Your* car?" Tyler said, still leaning against the hood. "You sure about that?"

"Yeah, asshole. Says so on the title."

Tyler cocked his head. "'Cause the way I see it, it's really my car now."

"What are you, on crack or something?"

"Bess told me you called her last night claiming you think you're Abigail's father."

Dan grinned, but his eyes were uneasy. Clearly, he hadn't expected Bess to actually tell Tyler. "Must piss you off to find out you've been sleeping with a whore, huh?" he said. "She was probably banging me the same time as you."

This guy was really asking for it. "Highly unlikely. But here's the way I see it. If you think you are, then you sure as shit owe us a lot of money."

"*What?*"

"Child support dating back four years. That's a lot of money I could use." He uncrossed his arms and pressed his palms against the hood. "And I see this nice car you drive, and I think, 'What the fuck? Why should you be driving this when I'm squandering my money to buy food for a kid you *claim* is yours?'"

"You aren't getting my car."

"Like hell I'm not. The courts will love to stick it to a guy like you. I'll get your car, and a whole lot more if I can prove you're Abby's dad and not me. But today, and today only, I'll make you a deal."

"What's that?"

"I'll just take your car."

"Like hell."

"Here's the thing. I know I'm Abby's dad. Hell, I've got the photos of me in the delivery room to prove it. But hey man, if there's even a slim chance you could be the dad, then I only stand to gain. So let's make a deal." He stroked the car, making his hand squeak against the steel just to annoy the guy. "I won't get a court order demanding a DNA sample from you, if you hand over the keys right now. What do you say?"

"I say your fucking crazy."

"Hell, yeah, and there's a whole battalion of Rangers who agree with you on that." He extended his hand. "Keys? Or do I get Abby and you tested and gamble on a lifetime income from you?"

"You can't do that."

"Funny, there's a JAG officer on base who seems to think I can."

Dan just stood there, mouth half-open, panic growing slowly on his face. Obviously he hadn't thought his plan through. He took a step back and tossed up his hands. "Fuck you, man. I'm not the kid's dad. Ask Bess. The timing's not even right. The kid's too young."

"Oh, I'm not sure I believe you. Why else would you call Bess up and risk my fist in your face again?"

"She pissed me off, man. Her living in that waterfront house. Hanging out with her rich friends. I saw those pictures of her and the kid at that wedding. Figured I might get her to give me something to keep my mouth shut about us. You might like my damn car, but you wouldn't like the payments that go with it. Thought I might get something out of her for a change." He paused, adding, "Even though she's not my kid, you know?"

"I'm not convinced." Tyler narrowed his eyes.

"Dumb bitch probably wouldn't even know the kid wasn't mine. She never was good for doing the math."

Tyler's fingers itched to implant themselves in this guy's jaw. Not the right time. Not yet. *Hold on, Ranger.*

Dan shifted on his feet nervously, no doubt watching Tyler's eyes grow more lethal by the second. "You can have your brat 'cause you're not getting a dime out of me, test or no test. If the kid's not yours, she's someone else's because she sure as shit isn't mine. You can't prove she's mine."

"I can get a warrant for a blood sample. I can have it by the end of the week."

"Fuck you, man. She's not mine. If she's not yours, she's someone else's. Not mine."

"We'll see about that." Tyler stood up, stepping toward him, and then walked past him, knowing Dan would try to coldcock him again when he wasn't looking. Tyler spun around to grab his fist mid-air and twisted it, throwing his own shoulder into Dan's gut, hurling him over his back and onto the concrete.

"Seriously? Dude, do you ever learn?" Tyler scoffed down at Dan's limp body.

"You okay over there, bud?" Mick called out, getting out of his car with Jack a few cars over, pretending they didn't know Tyler.

Right on cue, Tyler thought.

"I saw that guy try to hit you," Jack added. "Want me to call the cops?"

"Thanks, no. Just some misguided fool."

Another voice came from a jogger on the sidewalk. Joe stood there, shirtless in his jogging shorts, looking more like an MMA fighter waiting for his next brawl than a Navy Captain. "You sure? I saw it, too. He came after you when you were turned. I'll be your witness. I hate assholes like that."

Tyler looked down at Dan, and spoke in a quiet, deadly tone. "I don't know. Am I sure? I'd love to bring the cops in on this. You've already got a police record. Why not bulk it up even more? Forget the fact that you're not my kid's dad. If I could somehow manage to convince the court you *were*, you'd never get within a mile of her anyway with your record and the way you beat Bess. Then I'd walk away with Bess, *my* kid, and *your* money. Sweet fucking deal for me."

Still disoriented and catching his breath after being thrown on the ground, Dan blinked hard, focusing on Tyler's gaze. "She's not my kid. I swear it."

"You sure you're all right over there?" Joe called casually from the sidewalk, while Mick and Jack also stood at the ready by their car.

Tyler nearly grinned. Just another Joint Operations mission. He didn't move his gaze from Dan as he called back to Joe. "Yeah, man. Thanks. I'm sure he won't do it again." He glared down at the pile of human trash on the concrete, and gave Dan a slight shove with his foot just to remind him how vulnerable he was. "If Bess or I hear one more word from you—ever—I will pull your blood out with a turkey baster to get your DNA if I have to. And if she is your kid, I will take you for everything you're worth, right before I make you disappear from this earth. You hear me?"

"Yeah, I hear you."

"Asshole," Tyler closed, putting his foot right next to Dan's throat as a threat, sorely tempted to kick him in the face with him flat on the ground.

But it just wasn't his style.

Bess sat on the dock, staring emptily out at the water.

"Bess."

A feeling of relief washed over her at the sound of his voice. But her heart was still gripped in fear. She turned to him. "Tyler. What happened?"

"Is Abby inside?" he asked, glancing back at the house.

She shook her head. "At Edith's. I was having a hard time keeping it together. I didn't want her to see me that way."

He sat beside her on the dock, resting his arm over her shoulder and squeezing. "He's as good as gone, Bess. When I told him I was after him for child support if Abby turned out to be his kid, he nearly shit his pants."

"You're sure?"

"Positive. I told him I'd pull his blood out with a turkey baster. Don't think he cared much for the imagery." Tyler pulled his uniform shirt off, revealing a t-shirt underneath, and draped it over Bess's shoulders. "Even if Abby wasn't his kid, he thought he could scare some cash out of you. Blackmail. He saw those pictures of you at the wedding and remembered the waterfront house and must have thought you came into some money or had friends you could tap for cash. He hoped you might pay him off so that he wouldn't spill the beans to me. Guess he thought I was the type that might bail." He grinned. "But I don't walk away that easily."

Bess smiled, barely, and shook her head. "No. No you don't."

"You don't seem happy about it, Bess."

Bess's shoulders slumped. "I'm afraid, Tyler. Afraid to be happy. I feel like he'll always be lurking in the background in my life."

"He won't be. There's no way a slug like him wants to be stuck paying child support, Bess. If you had seen his face, you'd be convinced of that. Be happy, Bess. You're free of this guy."

She turned to him and gazed into his eyes. "You're really sure?"

"I am. Look, you might think that Abby is a reason for him to stay in your life. But he sees Abby as a reason to stay the hell away from you. He doesn't want anything to do with her, Bess. He doesn't want her."

Relief seeped into Bess's heart. It made sense. Dan didn't see Abby as the precious gift she was. He didn't want to be saddled with any responsibilities that came from a kid he never wanted. But could she dare to be happy right now, after living in fear for so many years?

"He doesn't want her," Tyler repeated, pulling her into his arms. "But I do." He paused, seeming surprised to hear the words that had come from his mouth. "I could adopt Abby, Bess. I love that little girl with all my heart. You know that. I could marry you and adopt her. We could be a family."

"What?" Stunned, Bess pulled away slightly from his hold just to look at him, all of him—his eyes, his face, his body language.

"We could be a family. The three of us. We pretty much are already, you know. You wouldn't have to work so hard. We could move down to Savannah next year when I return to the Rangers. There are a couple good culinary schools down there. I checked. Abby could go to day care right on base. It'd be a good life, Bess. We might not be living on the water right away, but I swear to you I'd never let you down."

The sting of tears filled her eyes. There was sincerity in the offer. She could sense it, see it in his expression. But something was missing. "Tyler. That's the nicest offer I've ever had in my life. Seriously. But—"

He pressed a finger to her lips. "No buts. Just say yes. Say yes and we can tell Abby tonight that she can start calling me 'Dad.' Do you know how happy that would make me?"

"I know. I know how much you love her, Tyler. It's just—you don't have to marry me just to know she'll always be in your life. I'd never stand in between you two." Her heart ached—not the feeling she would have expected after receiving a marriage proposal from a man she desperately loved.

"I'm not asking you to marry me just to keep her in my life, Bess."

Her gut twisted, resisting temptation. "Tyler, it's a generous offer," she finally said. "But—"

Standing, he shrugged. "Well, just an idea. Something to think about," he said, cutting off what she had wanted to say.

But I love you too much to see you settle.

But I want someone to marry me because he loves me as much as he loves my little girl.

But you've never even told me that you love me.

Was she being selfless, protecting him from being trapped in a marriage only to be the father of her little girl?

Or was she being selfish, holding out for a time when a man might propose with as much love in his eyes for her, as her best friends had from their husbands?

"I'll go pick up Abby," he said, leaving her on the dock by herself, alone with her tears.

Tyler climbed into his car, feeling a dull ache in his gut. He had never proposed to a woman before, but he had sat through enough chick flicks to know that it wasn't supposed to go like that. Bess was supposed to be dripping in happy tears, texting her friends, and envisioning herself in white. Instead, she had looked at him like he had just sprouted a third eye in the middle of his forehead.

What the hell?

He hadn't expected the proposal to slip from his mouth today. Sure, the idea had been brewing in his head the past few weeks. But sitting on the dock with her, with that miserable asshole finally out of their lives, it just seemed like the appropriate time.

Pulling into Edith's driveway, he paused momentarily before getting out of the car. So Bess didn't think marriage was a good idea right now. Fine. He could deal with that. It had taken him two tries to get through Ranger school. The first time he had broken his ankle in two places watching it swell to three times its size. It had killed him to have to pull out at the time. But he wasn't given a choice.

He went back for seconds the first chance he had. And that time, he made it through.

So if it took another try to convince Bess to be a family with him, then so be it. He never shied away from a challenge.

He walked up to Edith's door and gave a little rap.

Edith greeted him with her usual easy smile. "Tyler, dear. Come in. Abby's still sound asleep from her nap. We had a playdate with the little girl across the street and she exhausted herself. How did things go with Dan?"

"Mission accomplished. He won't be bothering her again."

She hugged him. "Well done, Tyler. Want me to wake Abby?"

Tyler opened his mouth to answer, but then snapped it shut. He could wake Abby up and be on his way in the next few minutes. *Or not.* "Um, can I ask you something, Mrs. B?"

"Of course. Want me to make you some tea? Or warm apple cider? It's finally the season for that, you know."

"No. But I could use some advice." He nearly cringed as he said it. What was he doing? He had only shared a few meals and about a dozen conversations with Edith. There had to be someone better he could ask. But if he asked his mother how to convince a woman to marry him, she'd be picking out china patterns for him by the end of the day.

Edith might be his best hope.

"Sit down, dear." She gestured as they walked to the couch.

The view from Edith's living room window caught Tyler's eye briefly. The Bay was calm, unlike his heart right now. "I, uh, just asked Bess to marry me."

Edith's eyes opened wide. "Really. Just this evening?"

"Yeah, I, uh, did."

She looked wary, probably noticing he didn't look like a man who was newly engaged. "And what did she say?"

Tyler furrowed his brow, trying to recall her exact words, but failing. "Nothing resembling a 'yes.'"

She eased back into the couch. "How curious."

"Why curious?" Tyler asked, daring to feel a faint glimmer of hope.

"Well, I don't think it would be wrong for me to tell you that she's been so happy since you came into her life, Tyler."

Tyler heaved a sigh of relief. At least she wasn't telling him he didn't stand a chance. "The thing is, I really love her and Abby, Mrs. B. And I think she feels the same about me. I know I'm just an Army guy and not really the prince that women fantasize about, but I know I could give them both a good life."

"I wouldn't undersell yourself, Tyler. You're an excellent catch for any woman."

"So, uh, why would she say no?"

"Well," she began, crossing her arms in front of her chest, "tell me how the conversation went."

Tyler relayed their conversation on the dock as best he could remember through the haze of rejection.

A smile edged up one side of Edith's mouth when Tyler was finished. "She must really love you, Tyler. I hadn't realized how much."

"Huh?"

"Well, any other woman in her position would have jumped at the offer. But I'm betting she loves you too much for that."

"Ma'am, you've lost me."

Edith laughed. "Think about what you said to her. You said you love her daughter, but did you tell her you love her?"

"She knows I love her." His forehead creased as he tried to recall a moment when he had actually uttered those words to her, and came up dry. *Crap.* How the hell had he let that happen? But she *had* to know he loved her. Couldn't she see it in his actions as much as she might hear it in three little words? "It's kind of hard saying those things with Abby around. We've been trying to keep it from her, you know?" Okay, so it was a lame excuse, but it would have to do.

"Well, then. She's probably thinking you want more to be Abby's father than her husband. Is she right?"

Was she? If Abby were out of the picture, would he still want to marry Bess?

Hell, yeah.

Edith sighed, tapping his knee. "Let me tell you a story about a friend of mine, Tyler. A friend from many years ago. Back in those days, we were taught to keep our buttons buttoned and our zippers zipped, you know. Of course, there were some who were the rebels back then. But not in my circle of friends. We were the good girls, you see. But every once in a while, one of us would slip. It happened to my friend."

Pressing her lips together thoughtfully, she stood, walking up to the window in time to catch a glimpse of a seagull slicing low across the sky. "We were in college, and she found herself pregnant. Of course, back then, you got married if that happened. Well, if you were lucky, you did. And she did get lucky. He married her. It wasn't a romantic proposal he made at all, but it was enough to get the job done."

Tyler stood to join her at the window, wondering where this story was headed.

"Two months later, my friend miscarried. It devastated both of them. They had so wanted that child. She grieved for so long—but not just because she had lost her baby. She thought she had lost her husband. She was convinced that he had only married her because she had been pregnant. Then for years later, they tried to conceive another child and never did. She felt like she had trapped him in a marriage he didn't want. It took a long time for him to convince her otherwise."

He stared at her, curiosity piquing. "A friend, huh?" He hadn't meant to say it out loud. "I'm sorry," he quickly said. "Not my business."

Edith smiled, her eyes filled with secrets that spanned decades. "A close friend. But don't worry. They had their happily ever after eventually. And it was well worth waiting for." She rested her arm on his shoulder. "So the only question is, are you going to have yours?"

He looked out at the tiny ripples on the water, sparkling in the low autumn sun. "You think Bess needs convincing that I love her for *her*, not just because she's Abby's mom."

Giving a nod, she cocked her head to the side, her eyes looking strikingly youthful despite her age. "Sounds like a fine challenge for a Ranger like you. Think you're up to it?"

He grinned. "Rangers lead the way."

CHAPTER 17

Nothing had changed between them, Bess reminded herself.

Tyler had assured her of that at least five times the past week. And from the way he was acting—seemingly content with the situation—she decided that her rejection of his marriage proposal was definitely the best thing for him. Even if it had broken her heart.

How tempting it had been to say "yes."

Life had continued as usual in the house, and Bess was too tired to even feel awkward about anything. Abby came down with a cold early in the week, bouncing back to her usual self again within a few days. Then Bess busied herself cleaning and cooking and preparing for the fifty or so people who would be coming over for a barbeque on Friday following Tyler's promotion ceremony.

"I really wish you hadn't gone to so much trouble, Bess," Tyler said, snapping Abby into the car seat.

Bess had literally just pulled the last batch of pumpkin cookies out of the oven five minutes ago. She had taken the day off work to prepare for the party, which might have been overkill, but she'd latch onto any excuse to not spend such a sunny day trapped in a dental office.

"I love cooking. You know that," she said casually. *And I'd do anything for you. Even stop you from marrying someone you don't truly love.*

What would it have been like, going to this ceremony if she had accepted his proposal? She'd be attending as his fiancée, not just his friend. Abby would have remembered this day as the day she hooked her dad's Captain's bars onto his uniform. Mick and Lacey, and Joe and Vi would be there to share in their joy. Even Edith was attending today. The only people absent were Maeve and Jack who had a bit of a harder time driving up here on a whim now that they had two kids.

It could have been such a memory for Abby and her. But now, Bess would always remember this day as the day she hooked Captain's bars on the man she loved with a fierce devotion—loved enough to let him go.

Wearing a new green dress that she never would have been able to fit into three months ago, Bess was feeling pretty good about herself, despite the dull ache in her chest. She flattened her dress out across her thighs nervously.

"You okay?" Tyler asked.

"I'm fine. Just hoping I don't make a fool of myself." Last night, they had practiced what would happen. It was a pretty brief ceremony. The Adjutant would read the promotion orders and then Bess would remove Tyler's old first lieutenant shoulder board with the one silver bar on it, and fasten the new one on with the two silver bars signifying him as a Captain. Then she'd lift Abby up so that she could do the same to his other shoulder board. They'd stay by his side while he gave a short speech, and then the ceremony was over.

Short and sweet. Surely she could survive that, couldn't she?

"You'll be fine," he assured her, touching her knee briefly. The sensation shot through her like a streak of lightning, singeing her heart. His touches hadn't been as frequent these past several days, and she could certainly understand why. He was probably trying to figure out where things stood between the two of them, the same as she was. "It's not like a Change of Command or something," he continued. "This is a pretty casual ceremony."

"If it's so casual, why are you wearing your dress uniform?"

He lowered his voice slightly. "Because I know what it does to you," he answered her cryptically, stealing a glance at Abby in the rear view mirror as she obliviously looked out the window.

The tiny hairs on Bess's arms stood on end. That was the first remotely sexual thing he had said to her in days. Maybe his final months here wouldn't be quite as awkward as she had thought.

After a short drive, they arrived on base and found a small crowd had already gathered at the historical tanks in front of the Fort Meade Museum. Not a cloud was in the sky, and the air was warm even though the leaves had started to fall.

Bess hugged Lacey as soon as she spotted her.

"How are you holding up, Bess?" Lacey asked when she was out of earshot of anyone else. Bess had told Lacey and Maeve what had happened the evening Tyler proposed.

"I'm fine. Really. Still confused, but fine."

Mick swooped in and laced his fingers with his wife's as they all gathered on the lawn. Joe had his arm around Vi's shoulder, despite the fact that he was in uniform. Bess felt a hint of jealousy creep into her heart, and she hated the feeling. Her friends' romances might have spoiled her for reality. Bess had actually heard Mick's proposal to Lacey on the front porch the day he returned from Afghanistan. Bess and Maeve had been sitting on the other side of the open window that day listening with tear-filled eyes.

Jack's proposal to Maeve had been no less romantic, but it was two days later when she finally agreed to marry him, waist-deep in the chilly waters of the Severn River with boaters blaring their horns in reaction to their romantic embrace. Bess had heard the story from Maeve too many times to count.

Then there was Vi. Bess got chills even from the memory of the day Joe had surprised her with a ring in Maeve's back-yard, after travelling from the Philippines. And the moment when Joe had said goodbye to Vi in the airport before he deployed—which had been recorded on a few smartphones by curious onlookers—was still going viral, even more than a year later.

Yep, the bar had been raised pretty high by the husbands of her best friends. And even though Bess never thought in a million years she'd have a moment as romantic as theirs, she couldn't dare say "yes" to a proposal made to her out of some sense of obligation or duty or need.

Tyler took her hand and pulled her to the front of the crowd. Bess never liked being at the center of attention, and today was no different. She kept reminding herself that no one was looking at her. This was Tyler's day. Holding Abby with her free hand, she stood at his side, proud to be there, yet somehow feeling a sense of loss for what might have been.

They could have been standing here as a family right now. She swallowed the lump in her throat and forced a smile.

A hush fell over the crowd as Tyler stood at attention.

"Attention to orders: the President of the United States has reposed special trust and confidence in the patriotism, valor, fidelity, and abilities of First Lieutenant Tyler Griffon..." the Adjutant began.

Special trust and confidence, Bess thought, the words striking her deeply. There could be no man Bess would trust more than Tyler. Her mind flashed back to the moment when Tyler first held Abby in his arms in the hospital. How terrified Bess had been to let him hold her precious, fragile child. Yet she had somehow known instinctively, even then, that he would be her daughter's protector.

"In view of these qualities..." the Adjutant continued as Bess's eyes were locked on Tyler standing next to her.

How long had she been in love with him? She couldn't even recall an exact moment when she had known. Maybe love doesn't always come on like a thunderclap or lightning bolt. Maybe sometimes it's a gentle rain that sustains over a long, long time.

Maybe it would be that way with Tyler, if his love for her might build slowly till the day when he could look at her with the same love in his eyes that she had for him.

She'd hold out for that day. Holding her breath all the way if she had to.

"...he is therefore promoted to the rank of Captain, United States Army."

Bess's breath caught, hearing her cue. She turned to him and, hands shaking, removed a shoulder board and replaced it with the new one. Her heart swelled suddenly, being a part of such a significant moment for him. She was so proud of all he had accomplished, all he had done for his country. All he had done for her and Abby.

Smiling at her beaming daughter, she scooped her into her arms as they had rehearsed, and Abby slipped the new shoulder board over the hooks of his jacket like a seasoned pro.

The crowd applauded. And in response, Abby cheered and jumped with glee after Bess set her on the ground, hamming it up in front of the many cameras and phones that were recording Tyler's first moments as a U.S. Army Captain.

Pulling out a sheet of paper, Tyler looked down at the words of his speech. Bess stepped slightly away from him, wanting this moment to be his alone.

"I had a speech all prepared thanking the many commanders who have mentored me over the years," he gave a nod to Mick, "and to my fellow Rangers and Soldiers." Shaking his head, he balled up the paper in his fist. "But it just doesn't seem to be what I want to say anymore."

Bess furrowed her brow, wondering what was wrong. For a man who had just crinkled up the speech he had been practicing for three days now, he looked way too happy.

Tyler looked up from the wad of paper he held in his hand. "There's this memory I had while I was getting my Captain's bars put on just now. It was about a year ago while I was on a Ranger mission, the one that earned me my second Purple Heart. I can't say much about it, of course, but I can tell you I got a hell of a scar out of the deal, shrapnel in my hip, and a good chunk blown off my calf. It hurt worse than anything I'd ever felt in my life—and I'd actually been shot once before. But this one was wicked. I was pinned down behind a Humvee, and I really didn't think I'd make it."

Bess looked at him curiously. He had never shared this story with her.

"They say that sometimes right before you die, you see the face of someone you love," he continued. "You know, your wife or girlfriend. Or maybe your parents. Well, I saw a face, and it surprised the hell out of me. Because it was this lady's face right here." He touched Bess's arm. "Bess Foster. I didn't know her especially well back then, so looking back, I thought it was pretty weird that I saw her face like that. But as I was lying there, watching my blood spill into the sand, I was remembering the day she gave birth to her beautiful daughter here. And she might hate me sharing this, but the sounds I heard coming from her delivery room—well," he glanced at Abby, "considering present company, I'll just leave it to your imagination. And then when I saw her, a single mom, holding her baby in her arms for the first time and knowing she'd never let that child want for anything, I thought, 'That's courage.' And so lying there, bleeding out, I somehow ignored the pain and found the courage to crawl to safety."

His eyes met Bess's. "I never told her that story, 'cause frankly it was strange to me to see the face of some woman I had maybe only seen four or five times and traded a few emails with. And the girl I was dating at the time would have probably been pretty ticked off to hear it."

The crowd laughed.

"But I wanted to tell her now, in front of all of you, because that was the first time Bess Foster became really important in my life."

Feeling the tears in her eyes, Bess's gaze dropped self-consciously to the ground.

"You see, I had always been wild about this cute little girl she has. High five, Abby," he said, and the little girl slapped her hand against his. "But I kind of overlooked Bess for too long. Way too long. Then over the time we spent together recently, I realized that she pretty much embodies every principle that I believe in. Every principle that's gotten me these Captain's bars on my shoulders. And those of you in uniform might recognize a few, because we talk about them a lot. Courage. Yeah, already covered that, so I won't tell you more graphic details about the delivery room."

Bess laughed along with the crowd.

"But also honor, integrity, commitment, loyalty. She's all those things. But that's not why I'm in love with her either."

He turned to her, taking her hand, and Bess felt a wave of goosebumps cover her skin.

"And yeah, Bess, I'm madly in love with you. I'm in love with you because you are the first person I want to see when my eyes open in the morning, and the last person I want to see when I close my eyes at night. And if I had my way, every minute in between would be spent hearing your laughter. Seeing you smile. And yeah, eating your beef bourguignon because it really is that good. It's that way now, and it will never change."

He went down on one knee, and Bess heard more than a few gasps in the crowd. Lacey's. Vi's. Edith's.

And her own—definitely her own gasp, as tears streamed down her cheeks.

"I love you, Bess. I don't want to—I *can't* imagine my life without you," Tyler said, his voice hitching as he reached into his pocket and pulled out a ring. "So, Bess Foster, will you do me the honor of marrying me?"

Her heart warmed at the love she saw in Tyler's eyes. Love for *her*. Not obligation, not duty, not a ploy to keep her daughter in his life. He loved *her*.

"Yes, Tyler. Yes, I will marry you," she cried through her tears, too overcome by emotion to even mind all the eyes on her right now, watching her fall apart at the seams.

Those in uniform in the crowd shouted "Hoo-ah!" followed by an enthusiastic round of applause.

Still on one knee, Tyler reached for Abby, "Is that okay with you, pumpkin? Can I marry your mom and live forever with you guys?"

"And be my daddy," Abby added, her eyes glimmering with hope.

"Yes, and be your daddy."

"Uh-huh," Abby replied with a squeal lunging into his arms as he picked her up, balancing her on one hip as he stood to embrace Bess.

Their lips met, and Bess's eyes snapped shut, concentrating, memorizing this feeling of completeness that heated her to her fingertips, and consumed her soul.

As their lips parted, they were swarmed by the crowd, stolen into embraces, and showered with good wishes. And when they climbed into his car to head back to the cozy house on the Chesapeake Bay, they were a family.

EPILOGUE

FIVE YEARS LATER

Boys are stupid. Abigail Griffon shook her head as Marcus Falcone pulled the string up from the depths of the Chesapeake Bay.

"You're doing it too fast," she admonished.

"I know what I'm doing," he retorted, darting a stubborn look at her before focusing back on the string.

She could see the crab in the water, clinging to the chicken neck Marcus had tied to the string. Half of her wanted the crab to hold on so that they could catch it in their net. The other half of her wanted it to let go, just so that she could be right.

"You're going to lose him, Marcus."

"He is not." Her Aunt Lacey's four-year-old son, Samuel always took Marcus's side. "He's been crabbing off this dock longer than you have."

"Have not," she argued back. "I crabbed off here when I was two. You weren't even alive then, Samuel. And you weren't even living here then," she finished, glaring at Marcus. The only reason she remembered it was because she had a photo on her wall back home—her crabbing off this dock back when she and her mom lived here with Lacey and Maeve.

That was before her mom and dad got married, and Abby officially became "Abigail Griffon."

Now eight years old, Abby couldn't really remember being called anything else. But the name still seemed special to her, especially when she put it on the top of her schoolwork, because it reminded her that she had a dad. A super cool dad.

He'd been away a lot over the years. Abby remembered that time really well, because they always had a big vacation right before he left. Disneyworld one year. Yellowstone National Park another.

But now he didn't go to work in a uniform anymore. Even though he worked on an Army base, he was a civilian, which to Abby meant that she could have her dad home on the holidays.

She liked that a lot.

"Well, I've crabbed off here a lot more than you have," Marcus said.

"Have not."

"Have to," he bit back, just as the crab let go of the chicken neck and disappeared back into the murky depths. "Damn."

Abby's jaw dropped. "Mom, Marcus said a bad word," she shouted, standing up and storming down the dock to Bess.

"I did not. I said, 'darn,'" he shot back.

"Did not. I heard it."

Jack stomped toward his son, stopping under the raspberry-covered arch that led to the dock. "Marcus, watch the language or you can say goodbye to your Erector set for a week."

"Okay," he grumbled.

Over her shoulder, Abby smirked at the sullen boy one last time before she plucked a pair of pink blossoms from the dogwood tree she loved. It had grown so much since the day they had planted it after Bess and Tyler's wedding. Abby put one flower behind each of her ears, proud that she had picked out such a perfect tree so long ago.

Back on the deck, she crawled onto Tyler's lap. She didn't care if her friends said she was too old to sit on her parents' laps. She liked to, anyway.

Tyler wrapped his strong arms around Abby like a giant seat belt. "Civilian life, guys," he was telling Jack, Mick, and Joe. "I'm telling you. You should try it. It was so nice settling on that house and knowing we could stay there as long as we want." They had just moved in last week to a little ranch house along the Magothy River about fifteen minutes up the coast from Maeve and Jack. "Jack, Mick, you're coming up on twenty years soon. The DoD could use you elsewhere soon."

"You're preaching to the choir here, Tyler," Lacey said. "Mick's already talking to some people at the Pentagon about a civilian job after he puts in his retirement papers."

"How about you, Jack?"

"No way. Now that I'm a department head, I'm sticking it out at the Academy till they start talking about moving me elsewhere. Then, we'll talk. After twenty, all bets are off."

"Admiral?" Tyler asked.

Even now that Tyler had separated from the Army, Abby noticed her dad still called her Uncle Joe by his proper title. She had asked him once why he did, and he had just laughed and said he'd probably call him Admiral forever.

"Doubt I can convince you there's life after the military, though," Tyler added.

Joe towered behind his wife's chair, massaging her shoulders as he talked. "Doubt you'd need to. We just put a bid on a vineyard in Northern Virginia. If it goes through, I'm putting in my retirement papers the next day."

The crowd seemed to suck in a giant gulp of air, and Abby couldn't figure out why everyone's jaws had dropped two inches each.

Maeve turned to Lacey. "Did you know about this?" she asked.

Bouncing her fidgety two-year-old on her knee, Lacey smiled. "I wrote up the offer myself."

"I can't believe you didn't tell us," Edith scolded.

Vi crossed her arms. "Hey, let up on her. I didn't want to tell anyone till the deal went through." Glancing upward at her husband, she shot him a look. "Thanks for letting the cat out of the bag, honey. I'm going to have your clearance revoked for that one."

Joe laughed. "Sorry I blew it."

A cry was heard over the baby monitor. *Naptime's over.* Abby rolled her eyes. "Babies cry too much."

"You cried just as much as your little sister when you were her age," Bess reminded her as she got up to pull Charlotte out of the playpen inside the living room.

"Don't," Tyler said, lifting Abby off his lap and setting her down on an empty chair. "I'll get her. You keep your feet up for a change."

Abby frowned. She loved her little sister, but it was kind of hard sharing her parents sometimes. Preferring a lap to a hard chair, Abby climbed onto Edith's lap.

"Oh, Abby, if you grow any more, I'm going to need a bigger lap," her Grandma Edie said with a laugh as Abby wrapped her arms around the old woman's neck and gave her a kiss on her cheek.

Tyler called from the doorway. "Can I get anyone

anything while I'm inside? Another drink? Edith, your glass is empty. More orange juice?"

"With a little rum in it again, yes, Tyler, dear," she responded with a wink. "Especially since you promised to drive me home," she reminded him.

"Consider me your designated driver," he answered. "And you're going to need one considering the rum cake Bess whipped up for your birthday. She made a separate cake for the kids, if you know what I mean."

Abby gave Edith a squeeze at the reminder of her birthday. "Wait till you see what I made you this year," she said proudly, firing a look at Marcus as he approached with Samuel in tow. The painting Abby did for Edith in art class would definitely eclipse anything Marcus had made, Abby thought. The little girl was nothing if not competitive.

"Well, actually, I think I have a bit of a surprise for you children," Edith said cryptically as Marcus and Samuel sat on the stair near them. "Is Kayla still on the phone with her friend?"

Marcus groaned. "She's *always* on the phone with her friends."

Since Kayla had become a teenager, she was constantly talking on the phone or texting her friends. She never wants to play freeze tag anymore, Abby thought glumly.

"Well, bring her outside. I have a little announcement I'd like to made."

Jack went inside and hollered, "Kayla, off the phone now. Your Grandma Edie has something she'd like to say."

A short round of bickering ensued till the reluctant teen finally emerged, followed by Tyler, holding Charlotte on his hip.

"Well, I've been having a few talks with Lacey these days," Edith began. "I've been looking at those waterfront condos they just built north of downtown. They have an indoor and outdoor swimming pool, tennis courts, even a motorized boatlift. And, after much thought, I just bought myself a three-bedroom penthouse. We settle tomorrow."

A silence fell upon the crowd, and Abby pictured herself swimming in an indoor pool in the middle of winter. How great would that be?

Bess spoke first. "Does this mean you're selling your house?"

Edith gave a nod. "Lacey just listed it today."

"Edith, are you sure?" Vi asked.

"Oh, more than sure. That house has been too big for me for a long time, and those stairs get harder every year on my knees. The only reason I kept it is because the extra space came in handy for the mids I was sponsoring. But I'm at the point in my life when I just want to spend more time with my grandchildren. And now with another on the way," she gave a little nod to Lacey's growing belly, "I can picture all of you coming over and making use of those nice pools. It's just a better lifestyle for me at my age. Maybe we'll get some tennis lessons for Kayla if she'd like."

Kayla, who had been glowering from the doorway till that moment, actually managed a smile. "Thanks, Grandma Edie. Can I get one of those short tennis skirts?"

Jack frowned. "Not too short."

Edith smiled. "You'll have to work that one out with your dad."

Vi glanced at Lacey. "That property is spectacular. The commission Lacey will make off that place will put her kids through Ivy League one day."

Edith chuckled. "Well, Lacey *has* been waiting a long time to sell my house. Even if the way she tried to get the listing was a little… unconventional. It all certainly worked out in the end, didn't it?" She sent Lacey a grin. "And seeing as I've got the best real estate agent in the state working for me, I'm pretty confident I'll walk away with an impressive profit."

Edith cocked her head to the side, a hint of concern in her eyes. "But what worries me most is that I'll get bored," she admitted. "I'm not exactly the type of woman to gather dust. So I was thinking I'd love to start a new project with the money from my house. Open a business. Kind of like a living legacy—a place that will carry on for a long, long time."

Bess sat on the chair alongside Edith and took her hand. "Don't even talk that way, Edith. We're all counting on *you* carrying on for a long, long time."

"Oh, Bess, I've got years left on me. Don't you worry. But I was thinking how much I'd love to open a restaurant. Right downtown. Maybe call it 'Mrs. B's.' Lacey and I even found a place I'm considering putting an offer on. But before I do, I wanted to find out if I knew anyone willing to run the place."

Abby's face lit. "You should ask Mama. She went to culinary school, you know. And back in Savannah, she worked in one of the best restaurants as a sous chef before we moved." Abby stressed the words "sous chef" proudly, knowing that Marcus wouldn't have a clue what a sous chef even was. "And she makes really good food. She's always wanted to open a restaurant."

Edith looked at Bess. "That thought had occurred to me. Bess, are you interested?"

Bess blinked back tears. "Really? Edith, are you sure? You could find someone with so much more experience than me."

"I doubt that. Besides, it's talent I need to make this work. Without it, it will never succeed in this town."

"Finally. Annapolis needs another good place to eat," Lacey said, moving toward Bess and touching her shoulder.

Maeve reached for Bess's hand. "Not good. It will be great. Best restaurant in town."

"What do you think?" Edith asked, her eyes shimmering

with delight. "You'll have complete control over everything, including the menu. I trust your judgment, and I'm too old and busy with grandchildren to stick more than a toe into these waters. All I ask is that we offer a good military discount so that mids can afford to eat a decent meal there."

A tear dripped off Bess's cheek onto her t-shirt. "Oh, yes. Yes, I'd love that. Thank you, Edith."

Tyler leaned over to give Edith a gentle squeeze around her shoulders. "Thanks, Mrs. B." He gave her a quick peck on the cheek and Abby was almost sure she heard his voice crack a little.

Edith waved her hands dismissively. "You'll be doing me the favor. It was time for me to try something new."

Heaving a bored sigh, Kayla interrupted. "Can someone drive me and Isabella to the Naval Academy for dinner?"

Jack looked at her. "Who's Isabella?"

Kayla's eyes widened. "Geez, Dad. Only my best friend in the world."

"*This* week," Marcus added, making Abby laugh in response.

Joe's brow creased. "Why would you want to go to the Academy for dinner, Kayla? Don't kids your age want to hang out at the mall?"

Vi angled her head at her husband. "Joe, wake up. She's a teenager."

"It's the uniforms, Joe," Maeve clarified. "The place is crawling with guys in uniforms. I hung out there any chance I could when I was a teen. But not till I was at least sixteen," she finished, narrowing her gaze on her daughter.

"Mom," Kayla protested, and Abby rolled her eyes knowing the whining would continue for at least fifteen minutes.

Lacey snickered. "And so, it begins."

As the sun touched the sparkling blue horizon, Abby

snuggled deeper onto Edith's lap, feeling cozy with her family surrounding her in the backyard overlooking the vast expanse of the Chesapeake Bay.

She might not live in this house any longer, but she'd always call this place "home."

FROM THE AUTHOR

Thank you for reading *Make Mine a Ranger,* the *Special Ops: Homefront* series finale. If you enjoyed these characters, you can continue to welcome them into your life as you read the **four-book follow-up series, *Special Ops: Tribute*** where you'll see lots of old friends. The first book, *No Reservations,* will give you a fresh perspective on some of the events you just watched transpire in *Make Mine a Ranger.* I have to say— it was so much fun to write it!

If you enjoyed this book, please help me spread the word by reviewing it. Your reviews are so important to independent authors like me, so I am deeply grateful for your support.

If you'd like me to let you know when my next book is ready, please contact me at my website to get on my email list. Thanks for your interest!

Completing this series has been a dream of mine for so long, and I never would have done it if I hadn't received so many positive reviews and thoughtful emails from readers encouraging me along the way. **You made my dream come true**, welcoming my characters into your life. I hope you have enjoyed this journey with me, and will let me introduce you to new characters in the near future.

I cannot thank my husband enough for his help with this entire series. You are my inspiration, my hero, and my very best friend. Nothing is ever real till I share it with you. Thank you for tolerating a wife who is so often pounding away at her keyboard and plopping manuscripts in front of your face to read when you come home tired at night.

As always, my thanks to my friend Chuck who, for four books now, has offered his input and Navy O-6 expertise only asking for second-rate wine in payment. You are a treasure. To Becky, who was the first person I shared the idea for the series with years ago. If you had scrunched up your nose and shook your head at the idea, this pursuit of mine might have had a very different ending. To my mom, thanks for reading my books even though I'm sure you're shutting your eyes through certain scenes. To Danielle, for your friendship and your sharp eyes, especially when helping me pick out a man for my cover. And to all the friends and beloved family who have offered their enthusiasm as I brought these stories to life.

Most of all, my thanks to all who serve our country and their families, who inspire each and every character in my books with their strength, courage, and commitment.

To all my readers, thank you again for supporting an independent author!

BOOKS BY KATE ASTER

~ SPECIAL OPS: HOMEFRONT SERIES~

Romance awaits and life-long friendships blossom
on the shores of the Chesapeake Bay.

————

SEAL the Deal

Special Ops: Homefront (Book One)

The SEAL's Best Man

Special Ops: Homefront (Book Two)

Contract with a SEAL

Special Ops: Homefront (Book Three)

Make Mine a Ranger

Special Ops: Homefront (Book Four)

BOOKS BY KATE ASTER

~ SPECIAL OPS: TRIBUTE SERIES~

Love gets a second chance when a very special ice cream shop
opens near the United States Naval Academy.

No Reservations

Special Ops: Tribute (Book One)

Strong Enough

Special Ops: Tribute (Book Two)

Until Forever: A Wedding Novella

Special Ops: Tribute (Book Three)

Twice Tempted

Special Ops: Tribute (Book Four)

BOOKS BY KATE ASTER

~ HOMEFRONT: THE SHERIDANS SERIES ~

When one fledgling dog rescue comes along, three brothers find
romance as they emerge from the shadow of their billionaire name.

More, Please

Homefront: The Sheridans (Book One)

Full Disclosure

Homefront: The Sheridans (Book Two)

Faking It

Homefront: The Sheridans (Book Three)

BOOKS BY KATE ASTER

~ BROTHERS IN ARMS SERIES ~

With two U.S. Naval Academy graduates and two from their arch rival at West Point, there's ample discord among the Adler brothers … until love tames them.

———————

BFF'ed

Brothers in Arms (Book One) - available now!

Books Two, Three, and Four
are coming soon.

*Sign up at my website at **www.KateAster.com***
to be the first to hear the release dates.

BOOKS BY KATE ASTER

~ FIRECRACKERS: NO COMMITMENT
NOVELETTES ~

For when you don't have much free time... but want a quick, fun
race to a happily ever after.

———————

SEAL My Grout

Firecrackers: No Commitment Novelettes (Book One)

Available now!

Novelettes Two, Three, and Four

are coming soon.

*Sign up at my website at **www.KateAster.com***

to be the first to hear the release dates.

Made in the USA
Las Vegas, NV
02 March 2021

18874795R00134